"I won't leave you here alone..."

Avery snorted. "I'm perfectly safe."

Not from him. Dawson had spent the day cursing himself for not giving in to his desires. He wouldn't deny the chemistry between them any longer, no matter how hot it burned.

Now he had to give her a reason to want him to stay—to want *him*...

He reached out and wrapped his hand around the oar she'd used to defend herself from an imagined intruder. Then he pulled it and her back toward him, as if he was reeling her in.

Her beautiful turquoise eyes widened. Maybe she felt it—the hardness of his body, the tension coiling inside him.

He should walk away now...run, even...from this siren who just wanted a story. But it was too late.

"Dawson...?"

"You're not safe," he said. "You're not safe at all..."

He lowered his mouth to hers, sweeping his tongue over her lower lip as the fire consumed him.

Dear Reader,

Hot Attraction is the second book in my Hotshot Heroes series for Harlequin Blaze. In the first book, *Red Hot*, insurance agent Fiona O'Brien took a risk and fell in love with Hotshot firefighter Wyatt Andrews. But she nearly lost him when he risked his life rescuing campers trapped in a wildfire. Fiona learned to trust Wyatt and their love to survive. The Hotshots learned the fire was deliberately set, and they have an arsonist on the loose.

In *Hot Attraction*, the Hotshots are still dealing with the arsonist's fires and trying to discover who he is without alerting the media. Big-city reporter and hometown girl Avery Kincaid knows there's more to the fire than the US Forest Service has admitted. For one, she knows Wyatt Andrews wasn't the only firefighter who rescued the campers—her nephews were two of the lost Boy Scouts. But the man they credit for saving them is Dawson Hess. She wants Hotshot Hess to get the credit he deserves. She also senses there's more to the fire. Dawson has an aversion to reporters but can't deny his attraction to beautiful Avery. He has his hands full trying to keep the town, Avery and his heart safe.

Happy reading!

Lisa Childs

Lisa Childs

—

Hot Attraction

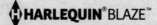

Recycling programs
for this product may
not exist in your area.

ISBN-13: 978-0-373-79892-6

Hot Attraction

Printed in U.S.A.

www.Harlequin.com

Ever since **Lisa Childs** read her first romance novel (a Harlequin story, of course) at age eleven, all she ever wanted was to be a romance writer. With over forty novels published with Harlequin, Lisa is living her dream. She is an award-winning, bestselling romance author. Lisa loves to hear from readers, who can contact her on Facebook, through her website, lisachilds.com, or her snail-mail address, PO Box 139, Marne, MI 49435.

Books by Lisa Childs

Harlequin Blaze

Hotshot Heroes

Red Hot

Harlequin Romantic Suspense

Bachelor Bodyguards

His Christmas Assignment
Bodyguard Daddy

Harlequin Intrigue

Special Agents at the Altar

The Pregnant Witness
Agent Undercover
The Agent's Redemption

Shotgun Weddings

Groom Under Fire
Explosive Engagement
Bridegroom Bodyguard

To get the inside scoop on Harlequin Blaze and its talented writers, be sure to check out BlazeAuthors.com.

All backlist available in ebook format.

Visit the Author Profile page at Harlequin.com for more titles.

With great appreciation for all the heroic Hotshots and firefighters who risk their lives to protect us!

Thank you for your hard work and sacrifice!

1

"No!" THE SHARP denial hung in the air even after the door slammed, leaving Avery Kincaid standing in the foyer, her mouth open with shock.

Laughter rang out behind her. "First time a guy ever turned you down for a kiss?"

"Two guys," Avery pointed out to her amused sister. "They both told me no." She watched through the window as her nephews ran down the driveway to jump through the side door of the van that had pulled up. They had wriggled away from her before she could give them good-bye kisses.

"Well, they're twelve," Kim said, her deadpan delivery cracking Avery up. "Not that that ever prevented you from getting kisses before."

"When I was twelve, too," Avery said. "Maybe eleven." She turned back to her sister.

Kim looked older than five years her senior now—older than thirty-two. She had lines around her mouth and eyes, a tension in her that Avery had never seen before. She kept glancing out the window even though the van—with the boys inside it—was gone. They'd just gotten ten a ride with a friend's mom to soccer practice.

"Are you okay?" Avery asked. "They're only going to be gone a little while." She wasn't certain exactly how long soccer practice lasted. She usually wasn't around to catch their games much less their practices.

Kim's eyes, the same turquoise blue of Avery's, filled with tears. "I didn't think they'd make it to become teenagers." Her voice cracked. "I didn't think I would ever see them again—hold them again…"

Avery closed her arms around her sister and held her trembling body. "It's okay. They're fine."

Avery trembled a little, too, as she remembered her sister's desperate call two months ago. She'd been getting ready to board a plane in Chicago and head home to Northern Lakes, Michigan. Then she'd been just a reporter preparing to cover the story of a wildfire consuming acres of national forest. After Kim's call, she'd been an aunt desperate for news about her nephews lost in the middle of that national forest. They and their Boy Scout troop had been camping in the forest when the wildfire struck with no warning and not enough time for them to escape.

"It's just so hard," Kim said. "So hard to let them leave again…"

It probably wouldn't matter how many weeks passed. A mother would never forget how close she had come to losing her children.

Avery squeezed her sister a little more tightly before releasing her. "They're fine."

Thanks to the special team of firefighters who'd rescued them from the blaze. She walked over to the coffee table where the boys had left their photo of the Huron Hotshots. Hotshots were a special team of the US Forest Service fire department—the firefighters who battled blazes on the front line.

Avery had included that in the short special feature she'd done about the fire. To write the copy for the feature, she'd researched Hotshots. But she hadn't learned enough. Her story had been about Hotshots in general, not the specific men who'd battled the Huron National Forest blaze—not the Huron Hotshots. Because they had refused all interviews...

There was more to the story—about the firefighters and about the fire. The tight nervous feeling in the pit of her stomach told her that; she had that feeling to thank for her career—for moving her from a small-town television station to larger networks, first out of Detroit and now Chicago. While the Chicago station was a national network, Avery wasn't on very much. She had to fight for airtime. And she suspected this story would make that fight much easier.

She wanted to dig deeper, cover the Huron Hotshots in more detail. Most importantly she wanted to find out what had really caused the Huron National Forest fire...

And maybe she could start by getting closer to one particular Hotshot. Maybe then he would grant her an interview.

She picked up the photo of the twenty team members. It was a press release photo—the only thing the US Forest Service had released to the media. The Hotshots hadn't released any information about the fire or the rescue. Of course they had been busy battling some more blazes. Fortunately those bigger fires had been in other areas. Northern Lakes hadn't recovered yet from the fire that had nearly taken the lives of so many children. And every once in a while another hot spot flared back up...

She shuddered as the nightmare returned to her, the knowledge of what could have happened had it not been for these men. She could have lost her nephews and even the town and everyone in it. Maybe that was why she kept coming back every few weeks—if only to stay a day or two—since the fire. Because nearly losing it had reminded her of how much she missed *home*.

But that was only part of the reason she'd taken a week off from the television station in Chicago. It wasn't to vacation, as she'd told her boss, but to cover what her instincts told her would be the most important story of her career.

The story was there—in that photo. In the one soot-streaked face that had caught her attention even before the boys had pointed him out. The grime did nothing to disguise his chiseled features—the square jaw with the slight dimple in the chin, the high cheekbones, the line of his supple lips...

She would like to kiss those lips.

The other guys were all grinning. But he looked serious—focused—his eyes the only lightness in his face. Were they blue? Gray? Silver?

She couldn't tell—no matter how closely she studied his picture.

"I should bring something by the station again," Kim murmured as she peered over Avery's shoulder at the photo.

"What?"

"I know it's not enough," Kim said. "That there's really no way to thank them for saving my kids. But I've been taking cookies and brownies to them when the Huron Hotshots are here in Northern Lakes."

Avery smiled. Kim was so like their mother, who'd headed up every church and school bake sale in Northern Lakes. Their parents had moved downstate when Dad traded his high school teaching job for a college position.

Apparently Kim had taken over for Mom. "You're thanking them with baked goods?"

"You have a better idea?"

Avery stared at that face—and the heavily muscled body that went with it. His arms bulged, his chest pushed against the thin material of his damp soot-stained yellow T-shirt. He was in the front row, so he was hunched down, his thighs straining against the pants that matched his T-shirt. Oh, she had some ideas how she'd like to thank him…

Kim had known her too long and too well. She smacked Avery's shoulder. "Hey! You shouldn't be thinking like that."

"I'm not married," Avery said. "I can think like that all I want."

Kim sighed. She'd been married since she was twenty—when she'd gotten pregnant during her sophomore year of college. Rick had dropped out and started driving a truck to support his new family. He was gone a lot. Fortunately Kim still missed him when he was away.

Avery had never missed any of her past boyfriends much after they'd broken up. But then she'd always been so focused on her career—and chasing down the next big story—that she hadn't had any serious relationships. She couldn't imagine being as settled as Kim was, in the same small town where they'd grown up. Or at least Kim had been settled before she'd nearly lost her children.

Her sister giggled. "They might appreciate your thankyou more than my cookies…"

Avery narrowed her eyes and studied the photo. "I don't want to thank all of them, just the one who really rescued them."

Dawson…

He'd only told the boys his first name. Kim had shared

that they sometimes whimpered it in their sleep, when they had nightmares about the fire.

"The Hotshots worked together to rescue them," Kim said. "They're a team."

The media hadn't focused on the team, though. They had focused on Wyatt Andrews. He was the Hotshot who'd disobeyed their superintendent's order to leave the fire. Wyatt Andrews had found the campers first, but he wouldn't have been able to save them on his own.

It was Dawson the boys had pointed out who had brought enough extra shelters for all the campers. It was this man who'd enclosed the boys in one of those special shelters with him. *Dawson* was the one who'd calmed their fears when they'd been terrified that the fire was going to consume them.

He deserved more than cookies in appreciation for risking his life to save theirs. He deserved credit for being a hero. And, if he was single, maybe a kiss as thank-you, too.

"THANKS," DAWSON HESS said as Wyatt Andrews set a pitcher of beer on the table in front of him, Cody Mallehan and Braden Zimmer. They had commandeered their usual back booth in the Filling Station, the bar around the corner from the firehouse in Northern Lakes. It was the home base for the four of them—when they weren't out fighting wildfires in other states with the rest of their twenty-member team.

Wyatt flipped him off.

"Hey, you know the rule," Dawson reminded his teammate. Whatever member of the team got interviewed or singled out in a press photo had to buy for the rest of them.

Wyatt slid into the booth next to him. "Is that why you dodge the press?"

Dawson had his reasons, and they had nothing to do with buying rounds of beer. But he pushed the past aside and just laughed.

"He doesn't have to dodge them," Cody said. "You're so busy hogging the limelight nobody's interested in the rest of us schmucks."

"Jealous," Wyatt teased. He and the younger firefighter had a friendly rivalry. It used to be over women— until Wyatt had fallen in love with a little redheaded insurance agent. Now it was over the job.

"It's bullshit," Cody said. But amusement instead of jealousy flashed through the blond firefighter's green eyes. He enjoyed needling Wyatt. "You and those kids would have roasted in that fire if Dawson and I hadn't come back and saved your asses."

Wyatt shrugged. "Hey, I offered to set the record straight but the boss told me to refuse all interviews."

Which Dawson suspected his teammate had gladly done. Like Dawson, Wyatt had probably had enough of reporters when he'd been a kid, too. The media preyed on tragedy. Now that they were adults, and had a job to do, reporters were a different kind of nuisance, putting themselves in danger to get the best shot. Dawson had had to rescue too many from nearly getting burned alive.

Cody turned toward their boss—Superintendent Braden Zimmer.

Braden pushed his hand through, or rather over, his brush-cut-short brown hair. "We want this story to die down," he reminded them. "And you all know why."

Wyatt cursed, and pitching his voice low, murmured, "The arsonist…"

So many of these fire bugs started blazes for the attention. They needed to starve him of attention, just like the Hotshots starved the fire of fuel when they cut down trees and tore out vegetation for the breaks. They had been successful in putting out the fires, but they hadn't caught the arsonist yet. And Dawson was pretty sure the guy hadn't stopped setting fires.

He didn't have the notorious instincts of their superintendent, who had predicted the big fire that had nearly destroyed their town. But he was smart enough to figure out that those hot spots weren't starting back up on their own. The ground had been too scorched and their breaks too thorough for that to be the case.

"It's not working." Cody confirmed what they'd all been thinking.

Braden shook his head. "We don't have confirmation that the others fires were deliberately set."

The superintendent wasn't talking about the hot spots, but the other serious blazes they and other Hotshot teams had had to battle. Maybe they hadn't been deliberately set.

Lightning could have struck a tree. Or a campfire hadn't been completely extinguished...

The Hotshots only knew for certain that the Northern Lakes fire had been intentional. That was where accelerant had been found at the origin—gasoline poured over dried vegetation, maybe hay bales. There hadn't been much left—just enough to prove that the fire had been no act of nature.

Anger filled Dawson at the thought of someone deliberately setting that fire and endangering all those innocent people. Those kids...

He remembered how scared they'd been. Hell, how scared he'd been.

He knew—too well—those shelters weren't always enough protection.

A low whistle drew him from his maudlin thoughts.

Cody had tuned out of their conversation, his focus on a woman who'd walked into the bar. She was all long legs and tanned skin and pale blond hair. She was gorgeous and vaguely familiar.

Every man in the place was checking her out. And she seemed to return their interest. Her gaze traveled from one man to the next and the next. She was looking, but she wasn't finding what or who she was looking for... until those greenish-blue eyes focused on him.

Her gaze holding his, she walked toward their booth. Those long legs closed the distance quickly, her heels clicking against the wood floor, through the peanuts strewn across it. She didn't belong in a place like the Filling Station—not with her snug blue dress and high heels. She looked as if she belonged on television—which made him abruptly realize why she seemed familiar.

Even worse was the way she was looking at him—as if *he* was familiar. Then she stopped at their booth and addressed him directly. "Dawson Hess."

It wasn't a question. She knew who he was.

Dawson felt as if he was facing the fire all over again. And this time he wasn't sure he'd survive...

2

AVERY WAS USED to everyone looking at her when she returned home. Reporting the big news in the big city—despite her limited airtime—had made *her* big news in the small town where she'd grown up. She was also used to men looking at her—usually with admiration. Not the hostility with which the men in the back booth were regarding her.

Apparently they knew who she was. But she extended her hand anyway—toward Dawson Hess—and said, "I'm Avery—"

"I know who you are," he interrupted, his voice gruff with irritation. "How do you know who *I* am?"

"You're a Huron Hotshot." She glanced at the other men. They were no more welcoming than Dawson Hess. "You all are."

"How did you know where to find us?" Superintendent Zimmer asked. His voice was even colder than Dawson's.

"The curly-haired kid who was washing trucks at the station told me you had all come here," she said. He'd also told her Dawson's last name.

"Damn kid," the superintendent murmured.

"I'll talk to Stanley," the blond firefighter said. He

slid from the booth, and as he did, his glance traveled from the top of Avery's head to her toes peeping out of her high heels.

She'd purposely dressed up for her trip into the village of Northern Lakes. But she hadn't dressed up for him. The man she'd dressed up for had barely glanced at her.

The blond guy shook his head and murmured, "What a shame…a damn shame…"

The superintendent slid out behind the blond firefighter. "As every other reporter has been told, Ms. Kincaid, the US Forest Service is not granting interviews at this time."

"Why not?" she asked. "This is a great time to bring more attention to the heroic work you and your team do." And especially to the heroic work that Dawson Hess had done. He had saved her nephews. And he deserved some of the accolades Wyatt Andrews had monopolized.

"I'm not giving any interviews," Wyatt said. The dark-haired man sat at the end of the booth between her and Dawson Hess. But, until he'd spoken, she hadn't really noticed him.

"I don't think she's interested in talking to you," the blond firefighter remarked with a deep chuckle.

"None of us are giving interviews," the superintendent told her. "We don't need attention. We just need to do our jobs."

She tilted her head and remarked, "I don't hear any sirens. There isn't a fire right now. I wouldn't be keeping you from your work."

But she wasn't keeping them at all. Wyatt Andrews stood up with the other two men, and the three of them walked out together—leaving Dawson Hess alone in the booth. Before he could slide out, too, she perched on the seat next to him. Not that she would be able to physically hold him in the booth if he wanted to leave. His shoulders were so broad that her arm inadvertently bumped his when she sat down. He was so muscular—big arms, big chest—that he could easily move her out of his way if he wanted.

"Please, give me just a few minutes of your time," she implored him. "I'm sure I'm not keeping you from anything."

Or anyone? She glanced down at his left hand. He wore no ring, but that didn't mean anything. She knew a lot of men—in professions less physical than his—who chose not to wear their wedding bands.

"Just because we're not at a fire doesn't mean we're not at work," he told her.

She glanced at the pitcher of beer in the middle of the table and arched a brow. "Hard at work apparently…"

Those light eyes turned out to be a pale brown—like gold or amber—until they momentarily darkened.

So much for sweet-talking him into granting her an interview or a kiss.

"We're not on duty right now," he admitted. "But we were discussing work."

They had looked intense when she'd walked up.

"I didn't mean to offend you," she said. "I was just teasing."

He shrugged, and his arm rubbed against hers. "You didn't offend me."

Heat rushed through her—starting at the contact with his body. Her dress had long sleeves, but they were thin and silky, so she could easily feel him through the light material. His arm was bare, the muscle taut as if he were tense.

All of the men had looked tense. Before the blond guy had noticed her, she'd noticed them—had seen their heads bent together in what had appeared to be an intense exchange. Over a pitcher of beer?

Why had they looked so serious? So preoccupied?

As Dawson had said, just because they weren't at a fire didn't mean they hadn't been working.

Her instincts were as trustworthy as they always were. There was more going on with the Huron Hotshots than a regular wildfire season.

And she intended to find out exactly what.

SHE HADN'T OFFENDED HIM, but Avery Kincaid had damn sure affected him—so much so that he hadn't been able to move as fast as his friends. He wasn't going to hear the end of that back the firehouse. They would tease him mercilessly.

And with good reason.

He wasn't like Wyatt and Cody. He didn't chase after every female who had a pretty face and a great pair of legs. Even Braden had let a woman mess with his head and his heart. Dawson had always been smarter than that—until Avery Kincaid had stared at him with those gorgeous eyes of hers.

Her beauty wasn't what worried him the most, though. She was smart and ambitious, or she wouldn't be working for a national network at her young age. Everyone in Northern Lakes bragged about the hometown girl who was making it in the big city.

"If I didn't offend you," she asked, "what is bothering you?"

She turned toward him now, so that her breast rubbed against his arm. And her knee pushed against the side of his thigh. Every muscle tightened in his body.

"I said you hadn't offended me," he replied, "I didn't say that you weren't *bothering* me." She was bothering the hell out of him right now. She was so damn hot that he felt as if his skin was sizzling despite the fabric between them.

Her mouth—wide and sexy, with full, shiny lips—curved into a smile. She leaned a little closer—maybe because it was loud in the bar, maybe just to tease him. In a husky, seductive whisper, she asked, "How am I bothering you?"

By breathing…

Every breath she drew pushed her breast against his arm. It was full and soft and warm. He struggled to hold his gaze up, to stop it from slipping down to her chest. But focusing on her face was just as dangerous. She was movie-star beautiful. Her golden skin highlighted her unusual turquoise eyes even more, making them shine brighter.

He'd seen eyes like that before—actually, two sets of eyes that had looked exactly like hers. So maybe they weren't that unusual. Hell, hers could have been colored contacts, but he was close enough—staring intently enough into them—that he would have noticed the telltale rims of the lenses.

She was really that naturally beautiful. His uneasiness grew, and he drew in a deep breath. Big mistake. She smelled of sunshine and wildflowers. Was it her or some expensive perfume made to smell like nature?

She leaned even closer, but thankfully she was much smaller than he was, so her lips were nowhere near his mouth. Just his throat…

He swallowed hard when her warm breath slid over his neck, as she asked again, "How am I bothering you?"

He eased back as far as he could in the booth. And reminding himself, he said, "You're a *reporter.*"

The media had made the biggest tragedy of his

childhood—hell, his life—even worse. They had exploited his mother's pain and his.

She laughed. "You make it sound like I'm a serial killer." But he hadn't offended her; amusement sparkled in her eyes.

"You might be as dangerous."

"Why?" she asked. "I only report the news."

He snorted. "Or you make news out of nothing."

"Nothing? That fire wasn't nothing," she said.

"No," he agreed. "But it was several weeks ago. It's time to let it die now." Like the fire had died—except for the hot spots that sprang up every once in a while. That was why, except for the occasional trip out West to relieve crews there, his team was sticking close to Northern Lakes—to protect the town.

"There's more to the story," she said.

He wasn't supposed to comment. But he hadn't been told not to question. And since he wanted to know what she knew—or suspected—he asked, "What?"

"You."

And he laughed, even as nerves clutched his stomach.

"I know," she said. "I know that Wyatt Andrews wasn't the real hero that day—you were."

He tensed. He hated that word—hated even more how easily it was used to describe someone who was just doing his job. He shook his head.

"I know," she said. "I have sources."

He laughed again. "Your sources are wrong."

"My sources were there," she said. "In a shelter that you brought when you and another firefighter found the campers and Wyatt Andrews. My *sources* were with *you*—in one of those shelters."

"Kade and Ian," he said. That was where he'd seen her eye color before—when those terrified twins had stared up at him as they'd asked him if they were going to die. *No*, he'd told them, and had hoped like hell he wasn't lying. "Your younger brothers?"

"Nephews," she said, and pride and affection warmed those beautiful eyes. "They are alive today because of you."

"Wyatt—"

"Wyatt Andrews didn't have enough shelters for all of the campers. If you hadn't brought the extra ones..." She shuddered.

He lifted his arm to the back of the booth, tempted to slide it around her—to offer her comfort. But the boys were fine. He hadn't had to lie to them.

"Everybody survived," he said.

"Because of you!"

He shook his head. "Because of the team."

"But you deserve to be personally acknowledged like Wyatt Andrews was," she insisted. "Let me do a special feature—about you."

At the thought of all those reporters focused on him, shoving mics in his face, asking him questions, he shuddered. He'd endured too much of that as a kid. "Hell, no!"

She flinched, making him regret the harshness of his refusal.

But he couldn't do it. He couldn't be hounded by the media again—couldn't have his life laid bare for all the world to see. Because they wouldn't be happy reporting just the current event. They would drag up his past and his pain...

"Why not?" she asked.

He forced a grin and told her, "There's nothing special about me. I'm just a man doing my job."

"A dangerous, heroic job," she said.

He shrugged. "It's not the only dangerous profession.

You have plenty of other subjects for your special features."

"But I want *you*." She reached out and brushed her fingertips over his chest.

Beneath her touch, his heart slammed against his ribs; it began to pound fast and hard. If only…

But she was playing him, just working him over so he'd agree to her interview. He shook his head.

"Let me do the feature on you," she said, "as a thank-you for saving my nephews."

He chuckled. "That's the last way I'd want to be thanked."

Her eyes narrowed for a moment, and she studied his face as if trying to figure out why he wanted no publicity. Then her eyes brightened as they sparkled again with amusement. "Well, I did have another idea of how to thank you…"

He knew he was going to hate himself for asking, but he couldn't resist. "How's that?"

She pitched her voice to that low, husky whisper again and leaned closer—so close that her lips nearly brushed his throat. "With a kiss."

He couldn't resist her, either. His heart hammering now in his chest, he closed his arms around her and drew her even closer.

3

AVERY'S PULSE QUICKENED, and her breath caught in her lungs as Dawson's arms tightened around her. He was going to kiss her.

But he lifted her, instead, right out of the booth. He moved with her and set her on her feet. Her legs trembled beneath her. Maybe it was just that her heel was on a peanut—maybe that was the reason. It couldn't be because she'd wanted him to kiss her, that just anticipating his kiss had weakened her knees.

No man had ever weakened Avery's knees before. Not even while kissing her. She had never felt an attraction like this. His photo had intrigued and interested her. But in person...

He was even more handsome. More muscular. More serious and tense...

She clutched at his arms before he could release her. "What's wrong?" she asked.

"Wrong?" He shook his head. "You're unbelievable. I've heard about you—the whole town talks about you."

She was aware of that. Kim told her stories—with pride and admiration. There was no admiration in Dawson's deep voice—only disgust.

"I knew you were ambitious," he said.

She supposed she'd made no secret of how badly she had wanted to leave Northern Lakes, where nothing ever happened—until the fire.

He continued, "But I had no idea the lengths you'd go to for a story."

She blinked and released his arms. She had apparently already given him the wrong idea, the wrong opinion of her. "Now you have offended *me*," she admitted. "I wasn't trying to seduce you into agreeing to that special feature."

His amber eyes were narrowed though, as if he didn't believe her. Or trust her.

"It was just a thank-you kiss…"

A muscle twitched along his tightly clenched jaw. That square, sexy jaw with a shadow of stubble on it. Although she was grateful that he'd rescued her nephews, she hadn't wanted to kiss him only out of gratitude. She'd wanted to kiss him because she was attracted to him.

He was so tall, so broad, so muscular. In heels she wasn't used to having look up so far into a man's face. He had to be well over six feet.

She uttered a regretful sigh. "Second time I got rejected today…"

He laughed. "I find that hard to believe."

"Why?" she asked. "You turned me down."

"I turned down the interview," he said. "Not you…"

Then his arms slid around her again, and he pulled her up against his hard body. His chest crushed her breasts as he leaned down, and his mouth covered hers.

She was supposed to kiss him. That was the thank-you she'd intended to give him. But he was kissing her, his lips gliding over hers. At first it was just a brush of his mouth, a tantalizing taste of passion.

She gasped as sensations raced through her, the attraction between them intensifying. Her pulse quickened and her skin tingled. He was touching her, too, one hand moving up her back to tangle in her hair. He held her head while he deepened the kiss. He parted her lips and slid his tongue inside her mouth, over hers.

She moaned as desire coursed through her. Her breasts swelled and her nipples hardened, pushing against the thin material of her bra and dress. They rubbed against his chest, and she moaned again, wanting more than a kiss.

He tensed and his head jerked back. His amber eyes had gone dark, his pupils dilated. His skin was slightly flushed. He shook his head and glanced around them.

And her face flushed—with desire and embarrassment. How had she forgotten where they were? That they were in a public place?

Because of his kiss…

She hadn't remembered lifting her arms, but they were linked around his broad shoulders. Her fingers had slipped into the short hair at his nape. It was silky against her skin.

Maybe he would be the one—the man she would finally miss when they broke up. Not that they ever had a chance of being together. They didn't live in the same city. And it was clear that Dawson had no use for reporters.

She didn't need a man in her life, though. She needed to focus on her career—on breaking the story that would guarantee her airtime. Even though her body ached for his, she didn't *need* Dawson Hess.

He released her and stepped back so that her arms dropped from his shoulders. Then he stepped around her, leaving her standing—legs shaking—next to that booth. Just before he walked away, he leaned down and murmured, "You're welcome."

"So DID YOU get rid of her?" Wyatt asked when Dawson walked into the firehouse.

He was lucky his legs could carry him; they weren't quite steady yet—not after that kiss. The passion that had burned between them was so hot he'd nearly gotten scorched.

He glared at Wyatt. The guy wasn't alone. Cody leaned against the truck next to him. It was a bright yellow fire engine—more likely to catch the attention of other drivers than red. That was why they wore yellow, too—to be more visible in the smoke and flames.

"What?" Wyatt asked. "We didn't intentionally ditch you with the reporter."

Cody gave him a pitying glance. "We thought you could move faster than that. You must be getting old."

At thirty-one, he was older than Cody. Probably just three or four years, but in Hotshot experience it was nearly a lifetime. For some, it was—a few years as a Hotshot was all it had taken to end their lives.

He feigned resentment and murmured, "I thought we never left a man behind..."

"That's the Marines," Wyatt said.

"It's why we went back and saved your sorry ass," Cody teased Wyatt. "You know old Hess here. He was physically unable to not rescue you and those kids."

Dawson glared at him. They all teased him about having a white knight complex. Sure, he'd saved a reporter or two in the past when they'd gotten too close to the fire. He'd even recently saved a girl from a bar fight. But it wasn't a complex; it was just part of his job.

Cody ignored his glare and grinned. "The reporter

must have figured out that you and I were the real heroes."

Wyatt nudged Cody's shoulder with his. "It wasn't you she was staring at."

"At least for once it wasn't you," Cody said with a chuckle.

"It shouldn't have been me, either," Dawson said. And he glanced around the garage area of the firehouse, looking for the kid who'd told her where to find them. Where to find him...

Dawson was the one she'd been looking for, and he doubted it was for a thank-you kiss. She wanted to interview him, wanted to do a story on him. But he doubted the story would be just about his helping to rescue the campers from the fire. It would dredge up his past, too. And dredging up his past might risk his present and his future. He could wind up losing his job with the Hotshots.

So there was no way in hell a kiss could coerce him to grant an interview. Even a kiss like that... He groaned at the thought of how silky her lips had felt beneath his, how sweet her mouth had tasted. He shouldn't have kissed her at all, because now he wanted to do it again.

"Hey, she didn't get to you, did she?" Wyatt asked.

Someone snorted, drawing Dawson's attention to the rear of the truck. Braden Zimmer leaned against it. "If anyone can handle the press, it's Hess."

Dawson grimaced. His boss clearly didn't know him very well. "I don't want anything to do with the press."

"That's why I wasn't worried about leaving you behind with her."

Had the superintendent not seen her? Of course, the guy was still hung up on his ex-wife. Maybe he hadn't noticed how stunning Avery Kincaid was.

"Yeah, thanks," Dawson grumbled.

"I knew she wouldn't be able to get you to talk," the superintendent said.

She hadn't gotten him to talk, but she'd gotten him to kiss her. Why the hell had he done that?

It wasn't as if he'd believed her sad little sigh and claim of having been rejected already. What idiot would reject a kiss from a woman like her? Not him.

But maybe he'd been a bigger idiot to kiss her—to risk her getting under his skin...

Cody laughed. "Hell, *we* can barely get him to talk."

Wyatt nodded in agreement. "It's like pulling teeth."

Dawson held back a chuckle and glared at them both. "Who can get a word in edgewise with you two smart-asses?"

Cody laughed harder.

"You are better at getting other people to talk than talking yourself," Zimmer said.

"See? It's your fault we talk so much," Cody said.

Dawson snorted.

"Did you get the reporter to talk?"

He'd gotten her to stop talking—when he'd covered her mouth with his, when he'd driven his tongue between her lips and deepened that kiss.

"Was I supposed to?" he asked his boss.

Zimmer nodded. "I wonder what she's doing back in Northern Lakes. Other reporters have given up. Why hasn't she?"

"She's a hometown girl," Dawson said. "And two of the Boy Scouts were her nephews."

Zimmer grinned. "You did get her to talk."

He shrugged. "She talks all the time—like all reporters. They love to hear themselves talk—just like Wyatt and Cody here."

Wyatt flipped him off.

"Get her to talk some more," Zimmer suggested. "Find out if she suspects there's more to the Northern Lakes fire."

She did. *Him.* But he wasn't about to admit that to these guys. He'd never hear the end of it. And it wasn't as if he was going to allow her to do a special feature on him anyway.

Dawson narrowed his eyes and studied his boss's face. "I thought the idea was to not draw attention to that fire—to the arsonist."

"We don't want to," Zimmer said. "And we haven't. Maybe that's compelled the arsonist to act."

"We haven't proved yet that he set the other fires," Wyatt said.

But maybe the other fires that had flared up in Northern Lakes hadn't been hot spots. Maybe failing to burn down the town the first time made the arsonist want to keep trying.

"He might act in other ways," Zimmer said. "He could have contacted a reporter to claim credit for the fire."

Dawson's stomach muscles tightened. "You think the arsonist could have reached out to Avery Kincaid?"

"She'd be the most likely choice," Zimmer said. "Like you said, she's a hometown girl who made it big. Her nephews were even in the fire. She has a personal connection to it."

And that was probably her only reason for pursuing a story that other reporters had let die. She was still upset about what had nearly happened to her nephews. Unless she *had* been contacted…

He recognized that tightness in his gut as fear. But it wasn't fear for himself. It was fear for her. If the arsonist had contacted her, she could be in danger. While the guy probably wanted attention, there was no way he'd want to get caught. If she dug too deep and discovered more than she should…

"And if he has," Zimmer continued, "maybe he's given her a clue to his real identity."

"But she would have run the story then," Dawson said. "It would be a very *special* feature for her." Much more special than anything about him. But it would also put her life at risk.

"She didn't get to where she is in her career without checking sources," Zimmer said. "She would want to confirm that the fire had been ruled arson before she'd believe some guy claiming responsibility for it."

She would. She might be ambitious, but she wouldn't have been hired by a national network if she wasn't good. Had she been fishing for information? If he'd agreed to an interview, was that where it would have led?

Cody uttered a sigh of feigned resignation. "I volunteer," he said. "I know it's a tough assignment. But I'll sacrifice myself to find out what the hot lady reporter knows."

Wyatt snorted. "I know your fragile ego can't handle it, but she's clearly not interested in you."

"She's not interested in you, either," Cody told him.

"Good thing," Dawson murmured.

They looked at him with shock—as if they thought he was jealous or something. That was so not him. He dated, but he'd never had any serious relationships. His job would always come first, and most women weren't willing to take second place. Most women weren't willing to get involved with a man with such a dangerous career.

Wyatt was lucky his insurance agent girlfriend had disregarded the risk of falling for a Hotshot. And even though a Hotshot from another team had recently died in the wildfires out West, she hadn't broken up with him. She loved him enough to accept what he did and the risk involved.

"Because Fiona would kick her ass," Dawson explained. Wyatt's hot little redhead had a temper to match her hair.

Wyatt chuckled but didn't deny it. He had fallen hard for Fiona O'Brien. Dawson wondered at his bravery after they'd all seen how their boss's marriage had crashed and burned. Braden's cheating ex was so cruel she'd even invited him to her wedding.

That was one cold woman. Fiona was nothing like her. Was Avery Kincaid? Would she be as callous with someone's heart?

He suspected she might—that what mattered most to her was her career. That was probably the only thing he and Avery had in common. But his job helped people. Hers could harm them. And herself. Her career mattered so much that she would probably willingly put herself in danger with the arsonist.

"I'll find out what the reporter knows," Dawson begrudgingly volunteered. It wasn't as if he needed to worry about his heart with her. He would never fall for a reporter.

Cody shook his head. "I'm not sure you're up to this assignment."

"I think he's up for it." Wyatt pointed toward Dawson's mouth. "That's not his shade of lipstick."

"You kissed her?" Cody asked, his green eyes wide with shock. Then he chuckled. "Maybe you're not as slow as I thought you were…"

Ever the boss, Zimmer jerked his head and sent both men off toward the weight room. They had a workout scheduled and had to keep in top shape for their job. It was one way of staying alive. Another way was not taking unnecessary chances.

Anticipating Zimmer's pep talk, Dawson assured his boss and himself, "I can handle this."

But even as he said it, he couldn't help but think that he was taking an unnecessary chance.

4

"YOU'RE WELCOME…" AVERY murmured as she walked back into her sister's kitchen. Her legs had regained their strength; maybe she'd just imagined going weak-kneed from that kiss. But she couldn't deny that her lips were tingling, that her skin was still hot. Even now—hours later.

After the Filling Station, she had stopped back at her house and changed from her heels and dress into tennis shoes and shorts. She'd thought about running but her legs hadn't totally recovered until she'd walked over to her sister's.

A few years ago she'd bought a cottage just around the corner from her sister's ranch house. Kim's place was perfect for her family, with several acres for the boys to run, a wide front porch and a big country kitchen.

"I didn't thank you," Kim said, her brow furrowing in confusion as she looked up from washing dishes in the farmhouse sink. She studied Avery's face and smiled, amusement twinkling in her eyes. "You look a little flustered."

Avery opened the refrigerator—not for anything to drink but because she needed a blast of cool air on her face. Not wanting to let her sister know how right she was, though, she pulled out a water bottle, barely resisting the urge to press it against her cheek.

"Did you do it?" Kim asked. "Did you actually give that Hotshot firefighter a thank-you kiss?"

"I didn't kiss him," she said, which was technically true since he hadn't given her the chance. He'd kissed her, instead. And what a kiss…

"Denied again?" Her sister gave her a pitying glance. "You must be losing your touch."

She was more worried that she'd lost her focus. She'd let Dawson Hess and his wicked kiss distract her. She hadn't gotten him to agree to the special feature, and she hadn't gotten any more information out of him about the fire.

Was there anything else to learn, though? Maybe it had just been a random wildfire—but it had started so early in the season…

Too early.

She remembered how the Hotshots had looked when she'd found them in that back booth—their heads bent together, tension on their faces. Something else was going on—something they didn't want the public to learn.

She hadn't become a reporter just because she'd wanted to get out of Northern Lakes. She'd become a reporter because she liked digging until she discovered the truth. She believed the public had a right to know. Apparently the Hotshots didn't care about keeping the public informed.

That irritated Avery nearly as much as Dawson Hess's little comment after he'd kissed her senseless. *You're welcome*…

But he hadn't given her the chance to thank him. Or to question him…

"I'm not losing my touch," she replied, but in reference to the story, not the man. Dawson Hess was part of that story, though, whether he wanted to admit it or not. Why didn't he want to admit it?

She hadn't met a man yet who didn't want to brag about his accomplishments. And Dawson had more reason than most to brag. Was it himself he didn't want the attention drawn to, or the fire?

If someone didn't want to talk to the press, it was usually because they had something to hide.

What was Dawson Hess hiding?

Kim sighed and murmured. "Uh-oh…"

Avery blinked and focused on her sister again. "What?"

"You have that look…" She shook her head.

"What look?"

"That scary determined look you get when you're after a story." Kim shuddered, as if in fear. "I feel sorry for whoever tries to get in your way."

Dawson Hess was the one who should be afraid. He had gotten in her way—denying her the feature, denying her the truth. The only thing he hadn't denied her was the kiss. But instead of letting her kiss him, he'd kissed her.

Clearly he was used to being in control. But nobody controlled Avery Kincaid. She would get what she was after—the story.

But was she fooling herself that the story was all she wanted?

DAWSON HAD SPENT the afternoon hoping for a fire call—nothing catastrophic, just a small campfire, a car fire, a big bonfire…

Anything that would have given him an excuse to put off his new assignment. But no call had come in to the Northern Lakes fire station. And there was nothing big enough happening anywhere else in the country that required the Huron Hotshots. Other crews were on the fires out West. Maybe the Hurons would eventually be needed to relieve teams that had been on the job too long.

But tonight he had no excuse.

So he crossed Rick and Kim Pritchard's porch to the front door. It stood open, allowing the evening breeze to blow through the screen door. Voices drifted outside through the mesh.

She was here.

Since he usually avoided the news, he hadn't heard her voice that much until the afternoon at the Filling Station. But it was clear and full and grabbed one's attention, making him want to listen to her, want to believe her. But Dawson knew better than to trust a reporter. She wasn't really interested in him—in doing a special feature about him or kissing him. All she wanted was information about the fire.

And he wanted to know why...

Had the arsonist contacted her?

"I met Dawson today," she said.

At the sound of his name on her lips—the luscious lips he'd so enjoyed kissing—his body tensed.

"Dawson?" a young voice repeated. "The Hotshot who saved us? He's not busy fighting another fire?"

"He wasn't today," she replied.

"Maybe he'll come by and see us," the young voice said. "He said he would when he wasn't busy."

Guilt flashed through Dawson. He'd made that promise to them, just as he'd promised they would survive the fire. At least he'd kept the most important of his promises...

He had been busy, though—with the fires out West

and with trying to determine who'd set the one in Northern Lakes. All of the Huron Hotshots had been on edge, waiting for the arsonist to strike again. They needed to stop him before that happened—before lives were lost.

He lifted his hand and knocked on the frame of the screen door. It rattled in the jamb.

"Someone's here," one of the twins said.

"Were you expecting anyone?" Avery asked, and her voice grew louder as she walked across the foyer to the door.

He'd thought she was hot before—in that blue dress. But in shorts and a tank top, the woman was nearly lethal. Her legs were even longer than he'd thought, her breasts even fuller. What would she look like in nothing at all?

His body hardened at the thought of finding out, and he barely managed to suppress a groan. Hotshots were on the front line of the fire, facing it head-on, so he was used to putting himself in danger. But he suspected he'd never been in as much danger as he was now—with Avery Kincaid.

Through the mesh her gaze met his, and her eyes widened in surprise.

"You weren't expecting *me*," he surmised.

She pushed open the screen door and uttered a small sigh—almost as if she were disappointed.

Hadn't she been as into that kiss as he'd been? Or had those little moans just been an act, a way to seduce him into an interview? Even though he'd suspected as much, she wasn't the only one who was disappointed now.

"I should have been expecting you," she said. "Men usually don't turn down—"

"Your kisses?" he interrupted. "So you were lying about getting turned down already today?"

"No," she said. "But I wasn't talking about my kisses—"

"Yuck," one of the boys said as he joined his aunt at the front door. "Hey, Dawson!"

"Dawson!" the other boy exclaimed as he rushed out from whatever room was off the foyer—probably a living room.

Dawson released the breath he'd been holding over visiting them. He hadn't known how they'd react—if seeing him again would bring the nightmare back for them. But they seemed genuinely happy to see him.

"Is she trying to kiss you, too?" the first boy asked.

A grin tugged at the corners of Dawson's mouth. Now he knew who'd rejected her kisses earlier. Of course it hadn't been a man. No red-blooded adult male would have been able to turn her down; he hadn't been able to and he usually had enough self-control to resist temptation. He couldn't believe he was actually attracted to a reporter. But after that kiss, he couldn't deny the attraction was there—burning hot—making him want to kiss her again.

"Tell your mother Mr. Hess is here," Avery told the boys.

One of them ran off to do her bidding while the other lingered.

"You, too," she said.

"It doesn't take both of us to tell her," he argued petulantly.

Dawson chuckled and wriggled his eyebrows at the boy. "I think your aunt wants to be alone with me," he said.

"Ewww," the kid said. "Don't let her kiss you!" As he turned to run away, Avery swatted his backside.

Dawson waited until the kid disappeared down the hall before asking, "Should I tell him his warning came too late?"

She glared at him. "*You* kissed *me*."

Yes, he had. And he wanted to kiss her again. Unlike last time, he resisted the temptation. He had to keep a clear head around her, had to focus on finding out what she knew without giving away anything *he* knew.

"It was your idea," he reminded her.

"Of a thank-you," she said. "You must have decided to take me up on my other offer."

"Offer?" Had she offered more than a kiss? Maybe that was what her moans had implied. That might be more temptation than he could resist.

"Of the special feature," she clarified. "That's why you're here, right. You decided you wanted your fifteen minutes of fame."

Was that why she had seemed disappointed?

"I thought that's what you wanted," he said. "To do a story about me." He had no intention of letting her do one, but he was curious why she seemed to have changed her mind.

She drew in a quick breath and nodded. "Of course. That's what I want—to tell the real story of the fire."

Real story? As usual, Superintendent Zimmer had been right. She definitely knew more than they'd released to the media. How?

Dawson would have to find out—without giving anything away himself. It was a hell of a fine line to walk, but working a fire was like that, getting close enough to set up a break but not so close that the fire consumed you. Maybe that was the key to handling Avery Kincaid. He had to treat her like a fire. Try to contain her without being consumed by whatever was happening between them.

"Wyatt Andrews risked his life to save those campers," he said. "That's the real story."

"So you're not here because you changed your mind about the special feature?" she asked.

He shook his head.

Her beautiful eyes narrowed. "Then why are you here?"

Remembering what he'd heard through the screen door, he replied, "To see your nephews. I promised I'd come by when I wasn't busy."

Her eyes narrowed even more, and she opened her mouth. But she didn't get a chance to speak before the boys were back with their mother close behind. He should have come by sooner to visit the twins. It was good to see them like this—happy and carefree. Not as they'd been that day when he'd zipped them into the shelter with him. Then they'd been shaking uncontrollably, overwhelmed with fear.

"Mr. Hess," Kim Pritchard said. "Have you eaten? I'm just putting dinner away but I'd be happy to fix you a plate. There are plenty of leftovers."

"I ate at the firehouse," he said. "But thank you."

"There's dessert," one of the boys said. "Peach pie."

"Peach pie," Dawson repeated with longing. "My favorite."

Their mother smiled. "I'll get you a piece," she offered.

But he shook his head. "I'd love to, but we try to watch what we eat during the fire season. We have to stay in shape." Their lives depended on it.

Her face flushed. "Then I should probably stop bringing brownies by the fire station."

"Don't do that," he said. "Your brownies are very much appreciated." Some of the young guys could and did eat anything. Cody, for one, would kill him if he shut off their baked-goods supply.

Her face flushed a brighter red. "It's the least I can

do to thank you," she said. "For saving them…" She wrapped an arm around each of her sons, squeezing them tight.

No matter how many weeks had passed, she apparently hadn't recovered yet from the nightmare of nearly losing her children. Her pain strengthened Dawson's resolve to find the arsonist—to see him punished for the damage he'd done and to stop him before he caused any more damage.

"Mom," one of the twins protested as he wriggled away from her. The other one leaned into her, though. He hadn't necessarily recovered, either.

"Dawson, do you want to see the Boy Scout badge we got for surviving the fire?" Kade asked.

At least he assumed it was Kade. During the fire Kade had tried the hardest to fight his tears. He'd succumbed, but it had bothered him more to not appear tough, as he'd thought he needed to be for his brother. Ian was younger than Kade was—by a mere five minutes.

Before Dawson could reply, hands wrapped tightly around his and he was tugged down a hallway by not just Kade, but Ian, too. They showed him every badge they'd earned in Boy Scouts along with every other memento of their young lives. And they did seem very young— younger than he'd been at twelve. He felt as if they'd brought him to show-and-tell; they showed him everything in their shared bedroom. Apparently their father traveled a lot and brought them back something from every city he visited.

He'd visited a lot of cities.

Dawson had expected Avery to follow them. But when he glanced at the doorway, only their mother stood there. Finally he managed to escape, after promising to take them camping later that week. When he walked back down the hall to the foyer, he discovered Avery was gone.

Kim followed him—probably to show him out. When she caught him looking around the living room, she uttered an almost pitying sigh as she told him, "Avery left."

"I see that."

Why? If she really wanted that special feature…

Kim seemed puzzled, as well. She glanced at the front door as if she expected her sister to step back through it.

Why had Avery left so abruptly? She'd said she wanted the real story of the fire. Dawson suspected that was actually why she wanted to interview him. But maybe she had another source. And what better source than the arsonist himself? Braden Zimmer could be right. Again. The man had excellent instincts when it came to his job; too bad he hadn't had them when it came to his personal life.

Dawson wouldn't make the mistake his boss had. He wasn't going to risk his heart on any relationship— especially one with a reporter.

Reporters rarely revealed their sources, but if the sisters were close, Avery might have confided in her. Maybe Kim knew whether or not the arsonist had contacted her.

"Did she have to rush off to meet someone?" he asked.

Kim's brow furrowed and she asked him, "Who would she be meeting here in Northern Lakes?"

"A man?" Arsonists were usually male.

Kim laughed. "You're the only man I thought she was interested in meeting."

"For a story," he said.

But Kim's eyes—so much like her sister's—narrowed speculatively. "I'm not so sure that's the only reason she's interested in you…" Then her face flushed a bright red as she realized what she'd revealed.

Dawson laughed. Avery wasn't really interested in him, only what information she could get from him.

But if she was attracted to him, Dawson wasn't certain he'd be able to resist her. Because he was so damn attracted to her, too.

5

AVERY WAS USED to people watching her. That was, after all, what a reporter wanted—to be watched. To get the most airtime. To get the best ratings...

But she wasn't on the air now. She wasn't even out in public. She was walking the road between her sister's house and hers, which was rural with just a few houses on her sister's side. The houses on the other side sat far back—on the beach of one of Northern Lakes's biggest lakes. Hers was just around the curve in the road, at the end of a long driveway.

Even though the sun set later now that summer had finally arrived, the tall trees blocked its light—making the day seem darker and later than it was. And colder. She shivered. She should have remembered how it got colder at night in Northern Lakes and dressed accordingly—the way Dawson Hess had been dressed. In jeans and a long sleeved black T-shirt. It wasn't his Hotshot uniform, but he'd still been sexy as hell.

Remembering how he'd looked, how his light amber gaze had traveled the length of her body when she walked to the door, heat flushed her body. She didn't need warmer clothes, after all—she just needed to think of him.

There was something about him…

Maybe she found him so attractive because he wasn't trying to get her attention, the way men usually did. If she were to believe him, he hadn't even stopped by her sister's house to see her. He'd come over to see the twins.

Was he telling the truth?

Did he have no interest in his fifteen minutes of fame? No interest in her?

She shivered again, but it was because of that eerie feeling she'd had since she'd left her sister's—the feeling that someone was watching her.

But who?

Nobody else was out walking. And the houses were set so far back from the road no one could have been watching her from their window. Were her instincts failing her? Or maybe she was just paranoid.

The trees thinned as she drew closer to her cottage. She'd painted the vertical wood siding a pale turquoise with white shutters and trim. As usual, she smiled when she saw what she'd had done to the place—how cute she'd made it. She didn't live in Northern Lakes anymore, but she'd bought the cottage as an investment a few years ago. Most of the time she rented it out to vacationers. But occasionally she used it herself.

She should have stayed at her sister's a little longer, or at least said goodbye rather than ducking out while Dawson was busy with the twins. But they'd been so excited to see him that she hadn't wanted to interrupt their time together. And maybe her pride had been stung a little that he hadn't come to see her. She wasn't used to men refusing her requests or her kisses.

Of course, he had kissed her…

Maybe that was why she'd left—because she'd wanted him to kiss her again. And she couldn't afford to be distracted right now. She needed to break a big story, so she wasn't reduced to covering fluff pieces. She wanted to be a serious reporter, not eye candy for the network. Was the fire a serious story? Was there more to it than had been released to the media?

She needed to find out—which was probably why she should have stayed. She should have interrogated Dawson Hess.

Her hand trembled a little as she reached for her door. The knob turned easily. It wasn't locked. She hadn't bothered. After all, this was Northern Lakes; nothing bad ever happened in Northern Lakes.

But the fire…

And that would have been a whole lot worse if not for the Hotshots. If not for Dawson.

Like Wyatt, he deserved to be acknowledged for his heroism. He deserved the special feature she wanted to do. But when she'd thought that was why he tracked her down, she'd been disappointed. She didn't want him to be like most of the men she'd known. She didn't want him to be arrogant and self-involved. She wanted him to be the true and modest hero he seemed to be. Hell, she just wanted him…

He obviously didn't feel the same attraction she felt, though. Was that just because she was a reporter? She knew the press got a bad rap for being nosy and relentless. But Dawson's aversion seemed more personal than that.

She pushed open her front door and a breeze caught her off guard. She must have left the sliders open to the back deck. The breeze off the lake pushed the curtains into the open area. The living, dining and kitchen areas were all one big room—all painted a paler shade of blue than the outside. The kitchen cabinets had been made out of wainscoting and painted a soft white. The furniture was all slipcovered in white linen—like the window coverings. And in that breeze, the long white curtains billowed like dancing ghosts.

She shivered at the breeze and at the faint scent she caught on it. Smoke.

Had someone been smoking inside her cottage?

Had someone been inside while she was gone?

And, if so, had they left or were they still here? Her heart beat hard and fast as fear rushed through her. If she'd been in Chicago, she would have had her Mace with her. But she'd left her purse, with the Mace inside, in the bedroom. Nobody ever stole anything in Northern Lakes. So she'd thought her purse—and she—would be safe. But now she gazed around, looking for a weapon.

There were no trees on the beach side, so the cottage was lighter than the driveway had been. But the curtains filtered that light, casting shadows around the open room. Doorways led off it to a bedroom and bath on each end. Someone could be in any of those rooms— waiting for her.

But why?

This was Northern Lakes. But she hadn't lived here in a long time. Maybe things had changed. Maybe bad things did happen in Northern Lakes...

AVERY HAD WALKED home alone. Her sister had said it as if it was no big deal—as if there was no risk for a woman to be out alone at dusk.

"It's not like she's in Chicago now," Kim had remarked when she'd noticed his wary reaction.

True. But that didn't mean she was safe in Northern Lakes, either. If the arsonist was in contact with her, it might mean she was in even more danger than if she'd been alone in a big city.

Northern Lakes was busy during tourist season. But this area wasn't within the village. It was rural. And it was getting dark. He hastened his step along the road she must have taken—the direction in which Kim had pointed him.

"Be careful," she'd murmured as he'd rushed off after Avery. He wasn't sure if she was worried that he might stumble in the dark or get hit by a car. Or was she warning him about her sister?

Avery was the one who needed the warning—to go no place alone. To be cautious and vigilant.

But if he warned her, she would know for certain that something else was going on in Northern Lakes. And she already suspected...

Hell, maybe she already knew for a fact—if she'd been in contact with the arsonist.

Had she really just been going home to the little cottage her sister said she'd bought a few years ago? He'd thought a woman as ambitious as Avery wouldn't have cared about ties to the small town in which she'd grown up. But according to Kim, Avery came home often—especially since the fire.

That was probably only because she was investigating it, though. It should have been old news by now. It was for every other reporter. Why not her?

He slowed his step as he neared a driveway. Was this the one? From the road he couldn't see the cottage her sister had described to him. He could only see a clearing going through the trees that was wide enough for a car. But the mailbox next to the driveway was a bright turquoise—like the house was supposed to be. Like her eyes were...

This had to be her place. If he'd been driving, he might have missed it, so it was good he'd left the Forest Service truck back at her sister's house. As an assistant superintendent for the Hotshots, he got a company vehicle. The super-heavy-duty four-wheel drive pickup might not have even fit down the narrow lane. Trees lined both sides and hung like a canopy over top of it. He felt as if he was walking through a tunnel.

And as short hairs rose on the nape of his neck, he also felt as if he was being watched. But if he couldn't see the house from the road, she wouldn't be able to see him from the house. So Avery wasn't watching him.

Who was?

And why?

Had the boys followed him from their home to see if their aunt might try to kiss him? Their mother had told them to get ready for bed, but that didn't mean they'd obeyed her. He hadn't listened to his mother, either, or he never would have become a Hotshot.

A crack rent the air—so loud that it sent birds flying from the trees. It hadn't been a gunshot. This wasn't hunting season, and this was, after all, Northern Lakes. It had only been the sound of a twig or branch snapping. But for it to have been that loud, the weight snapping that branch had to have been substantial. More than a twelve-year-old boy.

No, the twins hadn't followed him. But someone had. And they were watching him. He thought about calling out, asking who was there. But maybe it was better if the person didn't realize Dawson was aware of his presence—especially if that person was the arsonist.

While he tensed, he didn't whip his head around. He didn't scan the trees for a glimpse of whoever had made that sound. Instead he continued down the driveway toward the house—toward Avery. He had to make certain she was safe.

Within seconds the turquoise cottage appeared like a beacon at the end of the drive. The trees cleared and the last glow of sunlight shone through the windows of the house—penetrating it from the west side, which was on the lake, through to the east side. He stood at the front door, atop a thick, fiber-like mat emblazoned with bright yellow letters that spelled out Welcome.

He lifted his hand to knock. As soon as his knuckles struck the wood, he heard a soft, startled-sounding cry emanate from inside the cottage. His body tensing with alarm, he pushed open the door with his shoulder and burst into the house.

Something hard struck his head and shoulder. He flinched but ducked as it whapped at him again. Then he reached out and grabbed it. Wrapping his fingers around a long wooden pole, he jerked it from the hand of the person swinging it.

Avery cried out again, but this time it sounded like frustration rather than fear. "What the hell are you doing breaking into my house?"

He stared down at the oar in his hand—the one she'd struck him with. The wood was so weathered and bleached that he could have snapped it in two. He doubted it had recently paddled a boat. Then he noticed its twin hanging on the living room wall. She must have pulled it down from there.

"I knocked," he said. Or he'd been about to… "I only came in when I heard you cry out."

"I'm not crying," she protested as she proudly lifted her chin.

"Sure sounded like a cry."

"You startled me," she said, her tone accusatory.

"By knocking?"

"I wasn't expecting anyone."

He held up the oar. "So this is how you greet unexpected guests? Maybe you should change that Welcome mat to say Approach at Your Own Risk."

She reached for the oar, closing her fingers around it. "I'll take that back."

"So you can hit me with it again?"

She tugged on it. "I didn't hurt you."

"I'm seeing stars," he said.

She leaned forward and stared up into his eyes. And he was definitely seeing stars. Well, one at least. She was beautiful, and while she was young, she was already quite successful, if not quite a star yet.

"Did I really hurt you?" she asked, her voice lowering with concern. She dropped her hands from the oar and lifted them to his head. Her fingers skimmed through his hair and down the nape of his neck.

His skin tingled where she'd touched him. And his pulse quickened. Hers was beating fast, too. He could see it moving in her throat.

"Why did you hit me with the oar?" he asked. "Who'd you think was coming through that door?" Had she lived in so many big cities that she was jumpy and paranoid?

"I had no idea," she said, and her distinctive voice cracked slightly with fear.

He narrowed his eyes and studied her. "You really weren't expecting anyone?"

"That's what I told you."

But was it the truth? "So you just stand around with an oar in your hands?"

Her face flushed. "When I got home a little while ago, it seemed like someone had been in here. I even thought I smelled smoke."

Smoke. His heart began to beat even harder. "You were smart to grab the oar."

"I carried it as a weapon when I checked out the bedrooms and bathrooms."

He groaned over the thought of what could have happened to her. "You should not have looked for the intruder," he said. "You should have run right out of here and called the police." Or him.

He would have come if she'd needed him.

"And reported what?" she asked. "The smoke could have come through the open sliders…" Her brow furrowed slightly as she looked toward the sliding glass doors—as if she wasn't certain she had left them open. They were closed now; the curtains pulled over them. But through the white linen the glass glowed with the last rays of the setting sun.

Why had she shut out the sunset? Or had she been shutting out something or someone else?

"You should have at least gone back to your sister's," he said.

"I can take care of myself," she said, and she was all prickly pride again as she lifted her chin.

"I took that oar away from you," he said. And finally he released it, tossing it down onto her couch.

"After I hit you with it."

"If you'd found an intruder, he could have taken it away from you just as easily as I did," he said. "You shouldn't have taken that chance."

"Says the man who fights wildfires for a living," she said. "Like you should talk to anyone about taking chances. Hypocrite."

"I know what a fire can do," he said. He'd learned at a young age—only too well—the destruction and devastation a fire could cause. "You don't know what an intruder would have done to you."

She shivered and wrapped her arms protectively around herself. Without her heels and fancy dress, she looked small and delicate and vulnerable.

During a wildfire, rescuing people in danger was part of his job. He wasn't on the job tonight. But it didn't matter. He couldn't fight his nature to protect. He couldn't fight his attraction to Avery Kincaid, either. Silently cursing, he reached for her and pulled her close. Her body felt small and delicate against his but also soft and warm and curvy.

She trembled in his arms. Then her hands clutched the back of his shirt. Instead of pulling him away, though, she burrowed closer.

"You were really frightened," he said, as he pulled her even closer. The thought of her being alone and scared had a pang striking his heart.

A breath shuddered out of her lips and warmly caressed his throat. "I just had the strangest feeling," she said. "Like someone was watching me…"

Someone was outside her house. He had felt it, too.

"Who would be watching you?" he asked.

She shrugged. "I don't know…"

"You weren't meeting anyone here tonight?"

"I already told you I wasn't expecting anyone," she reminded him.

"You haven't been talking to anyone in Northern Lakes about a story?"

"Just you," she replied, her eyes full of suspicion.

"I was at your sister's," he reminded her, "looking at every single little thing your nephews own."

Her lips curved into a slight smile.

"You haven't been talking to anyone else? No sources?"

Her brow furrowed now. "My nephews are my sources," she reminded him. "They're the ones who told me that you were the one who saved them."

It sounded as though she was telling the truth. But Dawson wasn't certain he could trust her. Reporters lied. They'd lied to him years ago. Women lied. His friends—Braden Zimmer most recently—had been through enough pain to prove that to him. But if he pressed the issue of sources, she would figure out that there was more to the fire, just as she already suspected.

"Do you have a stalker?" he asked. "An obsessed fan?"

"I don't know if I'd call them fans," she remarked, almost modestly. "But I have people who send stuff to the station for me. Letters. Gifts."

Of course she did. As beautiful as she was, she probably got marriage proposals and jewelry.

"But I wouldn't call any of them obsessed," she said. "And not a one of them would know that I'm in Northern Lakes right now."

Unless they were already in Northern Lakes. Like the arsonist.

But she was right. They couldn't call the police. They had no proof that anyone had been inside her house. No evidence that anyone was watching her. Only that feeling…

One they shared.

If there had been someone inside, they might come back. Dawson couldn't leave knowing that Avery could be in danger. It would be against his nature.

"I'm staying here tonight," he said.

6

SHOCK GRIPPED AVERY. Earlier that day he had refused her kiss, but now he was calmly telling her that he was spending the night. With her. Uninvited.

Avery pulled back, tugging herself out of Dawson's strong arms. But she immediately missed his warmth as her skin chilled again—even though it wasn't as cold inside as when she'd first come home. She had shut the sliding glass doors and locked them. She should have locked the front door, too. So that Dawson hadn't been able to get inside.

That was why a cry had slipped through her lips when he'd knocked. Until then she hadn't realized she'd left it unlocked. That she'd left herself unprotected if the person who'd been inside her cottage had returned…

"What did you just say?" she asked again. Maybe she'd heard him wrong. She must have.

"I'm staying here tonight," he replied matter-of-factly.

"Do I need to hit you with the oar again?" But he'd already taken it away from her—easily. The way an intruder could have if she had actually found one inside the cottage. He was right about that.

"Maybe you should," Dawson agreed. "I probably need to have some sense knocked into me."

"Well, at least you know your suggestion is crazy."

"It's not a suggestion," he said. "I *am* staying here tonight."

"No." She would be able to rest easier with an intruder in her house than with Dawson there. If they hadn't been in a crowded bar when he'd kissed her earlier, she wasn't certain what would have happened.

Or maybe she was…

He shook his head. "I'm not leaving you here alone."

She hadn't felt alone—even before he'd arrived. While she hadn't found anyone hiding in the bedrooms or baths, she'd still had that eerie feeling someone was watching her.

"Why not?" she asked. "Why do you care whether or not I'm alone?"

Her family didn't worry about her. No matter how big the city she lived in, they trusted her to take care of herself. Her sister and parents knew how strong and determined she was. Dawson didn't. But why would he care? He'd only just met her.

"You're obviously scared," he said.

Or maybe he did know her. But she was overreacting. She had to be.

"Yeah," she agreed, "I'm scared that you're refusing to leave." Not because she was afraid of him but of what she might do with him. She was still too busy for a relationship—too busy trying to build a career to risk the distraction of a serious involvement.

He stepped closer, his amber eyes intense as he stared down at her. He stood so close that his chest nearly touched her breasts.

Her breath caught in her throat. He was so good-looking. So sexy...

Why was she protesting his staying? She didn't have to have a relationship with him—serious or otherwise. She could just have a little fun for once.

He leaned down, his handsome face drawing closer, his mouth just a breath away. And he said, "I want to stay to protect you. Not to sleep with you."

Her pride stinging again, she glared at him. "You're not doing either."

"Avery—"

"Why do you think I need protection?" she wondered, and she narrowed her eyes to study his face. "This is Northern Lakes. The most serious crime that has ever happened here is kids smashing mailboxes. Unless..."

Unless the fire hadn't been an act of nature. Unless someone had set it...

Why else would a firefighter be concerned about her safety?

"It's tourist season," Dawson said. "Most of the cottages on this lake are rented out to strangers. You don't have any idea who could be staying next to you."

That was true. But she didn't think that was the real reason Dawson was insisting on protecting her.

"I will lock the doors and sleep with the oar," she said. "I'll be fine." And it wasn't like the other cottages were that close. Although maybe that wasn't a good thing. If they were closer, she wouldn't be as isolated.

"Or you could go stay at your sister's," he suggested. "If you really don't want me to stay with you..."

As close as he was standing, as sexy as he looked and smelled, she had already started to change her mind about his staying. Maybe she'd rather sleep with him than the oar. But he wasn't offering to do anything other than protect her. But that was good. She couldn't risk the attraction between them leading to something more, something that might distract her from what really mattered—the story. She was certain there was one now. But what was it?

"I don't want to worry Kim and the boys," she said. Or endanger them.

Not that she was in danger. She was probably just being paranoid. And his concern was compounding that paranoia. Why was he concerned though? What did he know?

"So you think there's reason to worry," he said.

She shook her head, and a lock of hair fell into her face. Before she could push it back, his hand was there brushing her hair from her face. His fingertips skimmed across her skin.

And she shivered in reaction as sensations raced through her. "There's no reason for you to stay," she said.

But then he stepped even closer and lowered his head. His mouth brushed across hers—back and forth—just a tease of a kiss. Then his tongue swept across her bottom lip.

She gasped at the sensation, and he deepened the kiss, his tongue driving inside her mouth. His hands slid over her, too, down her back to her hips, which he clutched as he dragged her closer.

She felt the erection straining against the fly of his jeans. And instinctively she rubbed against it.

A groan slipped through his lips—into her mouth. She echoed it with a moan as desire overwhelmed her.

He lifted his head, pulling his mouth from hers, and asked, "Is there still no reason for me to stay?"

SOMETHING HARD DUG into Dawson's back and shoulder. It was like sleeping with a damn board. Then he remembered…and reached behind him and pulled the oar from the couch on which he lay.

How had he wound up here? Sure, it had been his intention to sleep on the couch when he'd told her he was staying. But after that kiss…

His body ached and throbbed, and not because of the oar or the lumpy couch. It ached from wanting her. And she was only a few steps away—secured behind a bedroom door. He'd heard the click as she'd turned the lock.

As if a flimsy bedroom door lock could have kept him out if he wasn't a gentleman.

Because he was a gentleman, he'd forced himself to pull back. Was that why she'd gotten so mad? Why she'd told him to enjoy the most uncomfortable couch she'd ever owned? Had she wanted him…as badly as he wanted her?

But it wouldn't have been right to make love with her—not when he was spying on her for the Hotshots, trying to find out what she knew about the arsonist.

Was that who they'd both felt watching them outside her cottage? Had the arsonist been inside, as well?

Dawson could smell what she had—that faint trace of smoke. It wasn't cigarette smoke, though. Or campfire…

It was more like the smell of a lighter—one where the flame had been lit for a long while. Maybe it had even been used to burn something else, like paper or cardboard. Unable to sleep—more because of her than her lumpy couch—he stood up and walked around the small cottage. There was a fireplace on the living room wall; the bricks had been painted white like the wainscoting on the walls and on the cabinets so that it nearly blended in.

The sun had set hours ago. Hell, it was probably about to rise again soon. But moonlight penetrated the white curtains, the way the sunlight had earlier, and illuminated the open area. He stepped closer to the fireplace and peered inside. Black paper was curled into a small pile atop the grate.

A click and a creak drew his attention from the fireplace, had his body tensing. Had the intruder come back?

"Are you cold?" a female voice asked. And Avery stepped from the shadow of her bedroom doorway into the moonlight.

She looked cold. Her nipples were tight little buds pushing against the silky material of her nightgown. She wore only a wisp of satin that clung to the sweet curves of her body. The gown left her shoulders bare but for spaghetti straps and ended mid-thigh.

Heat flooded him, pooling in his groin. "Cold?"

"Aren't you starting a fire?" she asked, gesturing toward the hearth.

He shook his head. "I was just looking inside—seeing if that was where the smoke you smelled could have come from…"

"But I haven't started a fire since I've been here."

She'd started something with him. The attraction between them was so hot. He couldn't remember wanting anyone as badly as he wanted her. Usually he had no problem controlling his desire. He wasn't like some of his fellow Hotshots. He didn't date indiscriminately. But he dated.

Just a few months ago he'd been out with a cute brunette he'd rescued from a bar fight. They'd only gone out a couple of times when they'd concluded they would only be friends. Maybe that was because the fire had hit Northern Lakes, though, and work had consumed him after that.

So she had probably realized he wasn't good relationship material. Women were initially drawn to Hotshots because of the danger of their profession. But when they realized how many hours they worked and how much Hotshots were out of town, they ended things. Absence had never made the heart grow fonder…at least not for him.

He suspected Avery Kincaid wasn't looking for a man at all. The ambitious reporter was after a story. And he was beginning to worry that she would find it. Or that it had found her.

"There are ashes in the hearth," he pointed out.

She drew closer and looked inside the fireplace. Then she shrugged her bare shoulders; one of the spaghetti straps slid down her arm and her bodice dipped low, exposing a considerable amount of cleavage.

His mouth went dry.

"Maybe the last renters used the fireplace," she mused. "But Kim doesn't usually miss anything when she cleans for me after they leave."

He doubted Kim had missed the ashes. They were recent. Probably burned just a few hours ago. Someone had definitely been inside her place. He was glad he'd stayed, even though his back—and other parts of his body—ached.

"Someone was here," she said, as she arrived at the same conclusion he had. Her voice a little shaky with fear, she continued, "I didn't imagine it."

He shook his head. "No. You didn't imagine it." And neither had he. Someone had been out there last night, watching him walk up to her cottage.

Who?

Some Peeping Tom? Deranged fan? Or the arsonist?

"Why would someone be inside my house?" she wondered aloud. "Nothing was taken. What could they have wanted?"

Probably the same thing Dawson wanted: her. He reached out and tugged up the strap that had slipped down her arm. But the satin did little to cover her body. Her nipples pushed against the thin fabric.

His body tensed, his cock throbbing against the fly of his suddenly too tight jeans. No wonder he hadn't been able to sleep. He should have taken them off. But instead of taking off his clothes, he wanted to take off hers.

"What could they have wanted?" she asked again.

He glided his fingertips along her shoulder, toying with the strap he'd pulled up. "How can you not know?"

She was beautiful. He knew she knew it. He suspected she used her looks to her advantage, to get people to talk to her. Dawson never felt like talking; he'd done enough of that as a kid—to reporters, to counselors.

But he felt even less like talking around her, and not just because she might report whatever he told her. He didn't feel like talking because there were so many others things he would rather do with her. Like kissing. Like caressing…

"I wouldn't ask you if I knew what they wanted," she said.

"You," he said. "Whoever broke in here could have been after you…"

She gasped. "But…"

"You're beautiful," he said. "You're staying here alone."

She shivered and stepped closer to him, as if she needed his warmth. Or his protection. "I'm not alone now."

"No, you're not." Slipping his fingers beneath that thin strap, he tugged her closer yet. Then he lowered his head and brushed his mouth across hers.

She sighed softly, her breath whispering across his

lips. And he deepened the kiss, delving his tongue into her mouth. He stroked it across hers. She tasted so damn sweet.

And while she'd been shivering moments ago, her body was hot against his. That strap slipped down again. So he pushed down the other one, and the entire top of her gown dropped, freeing her breasts. Moonlight bathed them, turning her tanned skin even more golden.

He cupped one of her breasts in his palm. It was so round—so full. Then he flicked his thumb back and forth over the distended nipple.

Even though her teeth had sunk into her bottom lip, a moan slipped out of her mouth. And she arched toward him, pushing her breast more fully into his hand.

Touching wasn't enough. He had to taste, too. So he lowered his head. He moved his lips over the curve, pressing soft kisses to her silky skin. Then he flicked his tongue out, and like he had his thumb, he brushed it back and forth across her nipple.

She moaned again—loudly. She was so responsive. So passionate. He closed his lips around her nipple and gently tugged. And she reached for him, her fingers tunneling through his hair—clasping his head against her breast. Unable to lift his head, he lifted her instead. He wrapped his hands around her waist; it was so small his fingers overlapped.

Her fingers slipped from his hair, and he finally pulled his head from her breast. She stared down at him, her eyes wide with surprise that he'd lifted her—that, held aloft as she was, she was above him.

On television she seemed larger than life—as if she filled the screen. But in reality she was delicate and vulnerable. So light that he carried her easily toward the door she'd left open to her bedroom.

She trembled in his arms—maybe from the cold. Maybe from passion. But he only remembered how scared she'd been when he'd showed up at her house.

He had stayed to protect her from whoever had been watching her—watching them. Whoever had already been inside her cottage, burning something in her fireplace.

Had that been a warning? Maybe it was one he needed to heed.

7

"THANKS A LOT," Kim said, as she stepped through the door Avery held open for her.

In a reversal of the day before, Avery blinked and asked, "What are you thanking me for?" Smelling the scent of coffee and cinnamon wafting from the basket in her sister's arms, she said, "I'm the one who should be thanking you. You didn't have to bring me breakfast."

Her stomach grumbled in appreciation, though. And just the smell of coffee began to clear the sleep—or, rather, lack thereof—from her throbbing head.

Kim set the basket on the polished wood counter and pulled out a clear glass container of frosting-covered cinnamon rolls and a carafe of coffee. "I thought you might need sustenance after the night you had."

She hadn't called her sister—hadn't told her about the smoke and the feeling that someone had been inside her home. "What are you talking about?"

"The hot fireman," Kim said. "I told him where to find you."

She wasn't about to thank her sister for that. Sure, maybe having him stay had made her feel a little safer.

But it wasn't as if she wouldn't have been able to protect herself had her intruder returned.

She'd been taking care of herself for years. She didn't need a man. She certainly didn't need Dawson Hess.

But her body called her on the lie as it continued to ache for his. Her nipples were still tight—still longing for more of his attention.

Even as her face flushed, she murmured, "I don't know what you're talking about…"

"He must have found you since his truck was parked in my driveway until just a couple hours ago," Kim said. "And I doubt a Hotshot firefighter who tracked down lost campers in the middle of hundreds of acres of national forest would have gotten lost on his way over here."

"He didn't get lost." But she had. She'd lost her focus. While she'd had him alone, she should have been interviewing him—about himself, about the fire. She should have been trying to get him to talk. But she'd let him distract her from her job—from the story. That had never happened before. But she'd never felt such an intense attraction before, either. But he obviously didn't feel the attraction—at least not to the same extent she did. Even though he kissed her, he always managed to pull back. Even though he touched her, he always managed to stop. Was it because he didn't find her as attractive?

When she'd heard him moving around in the living room, she'd slipped out of her old T-shirt and boxers and into that silky nightgown. She'd wanted to tease him. She'd wanted him to want her.

The pressure he'd built inside her—with his hand on her breast, then his lips and his tongue…

It wound even tighter now. Her hand shook as she reached for the cup of coffee her sister held out to her.

She probably didn't need the caffeine—except that she was exhausted.

"You look like you didn't sleep at all," her sister observed as Kim sipped at her own cup of coffee.

"I didn't."

"He's that good?" Kim asked with a wistful sigh.

Maybe that was what he thought—that he'd been a good guy when he'd laid her on her bed and walked away. Maybe he'd thought he was doing the right thing.

Jerk…

"I wouldn't know," Avery bitterly admitted.

Kim laughed. "Seriously? Nothing happened?"

She might not have been as achy if *nothing* had happened. But his kisses—his touch—had turned up the heat. She was more hot and bothered than she could ever remember being.

She shook her head.

"Then why'd he stay all night?"

She tensed. She didn't want to worry her sister. But she had to know. Gesturing toward the fireplace, Avery asked, "Were the ashes in it from the last renters?"

"There are ashes in it?" Kim asked. She walked over to it and looked inside. Then she shrugged. "I don't know."

"Don't you usually clean it?"

"I didn't think to look in it," she admitted. "The weather's been unseasonably warm. I probably didn't think anyone had used it."

Avery expelled a slight breath of relief. "That's good…"

"Did you think someone had been in here while you were at my house?" Kim asked. And she glanced nervously around.

Avery shrugged. "I hadn't locked the door when I left. And then when I came inside, it smelled like smoke…"

"There were bonfires last night," Kim said. "The Ahearnes and the Stovers both had one."

Their cottages were down the beach, but close enough that Avery could have smelled their fires.

Her face flushed again—with embarrassment that she'd overreacted.

"This is Northern Lakes," her sister said. "Not Chicago. You're safe here."

Avery nodded. "Of course. I know that…"

"So you just acted scared to get our local hero to spend the night?" Kim teased.

Pride lifted Avery's chin. "I am no damsel in distress."

And maybe that was the problem with Dawson. Maybe he liked helpless women he could rescue, so he could play the hero.

"I said *acted* scared," Kim said. "I know you're not. You'd have no reason to really be afraid."

Remembering that eerie sensation of being watched and the smell of smoke, Avery shivered. She wasn't so certain that was true. But why would she be in any danger?

Sure, she was asking questions about the fire. But the only people who had seemed to be upset about that were the Hotshots. Going after a story had put her in danger in the past, though. When she'd worked in Detroit, she'd investigated a string of fires, and the gangs who'd been setting them on each other's turf had threatened her life.

But her life hadn't been threatened last night. She wasn't even certain someone had been inside her cottage.

"I'm not afraid," Avery said. But she wasn't stupid, either, so she would be cautious. She already suspected there was more to the fire than had been revealed to the public. Could it have been an arson? Northern Lakes didn't have gangs, but it might have one very disturbed person…

Who could have been inside her home…

She shivered again.

"So I shouldn't have told the hot firefighter where to find you?" Kim asked.

If he hadn't found her, Avery wouldn't be deliciously on edge from his kisses—from his touch. "No," she replied. "No wonder you brought the cinnamon rolls. It was out of guilt." She pulled one out of the glass bowl and took a big bite. At least her sister's guilt tasted sweet and was all gooey, cinnamon-flavored goodness.

"All he wanted was to make sure you got safely home. He saved my kids' lives," Kim said. And the teasing was gone now. "I feel like I owe him."

"I love Ian and Kade, too," Avery said. She'd only been fifteen when they'd been born, but her sister had wanted her in the delivery room. Seeing the agony Kim had endured had made her even more determined to avoid teen pregnancy—or pregnancy at any age. But being one of the first to see and hold the twins had built a special bond with them—another reason she was determined to investigate the fire that had nearly killed them.

"I am surprised he cared if I got safely home or not. Dawson is not a fan of reporters." In general? Or her in particular? Maybe he'd heard about her story on the arsons in Detroit. One of the firefighters she'd interviewed there worked as a Hotshot during wildfire season.

"So, nothing really happened last night?" Kim asked skeptically. "All night?"

Trying to forget about those kisses and how he'd touched her, Avery shook her head.

Kim uttered a sigh of disappointment.

"Why do you care?" she asked.

"Now I can't grill you for details about how he was," Kim said.

"You wanted to live vicariously through me?" Her sister really had settled down too soon.

Kim shook her head. "No. But since the US Forest Service truck was parked in my driveway all night, I'm the one everyone's going to be talking about."

Avery sucked in a breath of shock. "I hadn't thought about that. Do you want me to call Rick for you?"

"Some of his buddies already called him," Kim said. "That's why I'm up so early."

Avery cursed. She'd forgotten how *small* her hometown actually was. That was why she'd wanted out so badly. She'd wanted to live in the anonymity of a big city and report about other people's lives instead of having people talk about hers. Dawson would probably call her a hypocrite regarding that. But she worked so much that she didn't have anything interesting for anyone to report about her. "I'll call Rick and explain everything."

Kim waved a hand in dismissal. "He's fine. He trusts me and I trust him."

"But you spend so much time apart..." Avery had wondered how their marriage survived the long absences.

"That's why it's so important that we trust each other," Kim said. "And we trust what we have. It's strong." She smiled. "Strong enough to survive a little small-town gossip." She lifted her chin and her smile widened. "Maybe it'll be nice to be the one everybody's talking about for once—instead of you."

"Nobody needs to be talking about me," Avery said. She wasn't the story. Dawson was. "Or you."

Kim wrapped her hands around her mug of coffee and shivered. "You've got that look again..."

"I don't care what he says. I'm going to do that special

feature about Dawson Hess," Avery said. "He deserves to be the one everybody's talking about, not just Wyatt Andrews. He deserves some of the accolades."

"Even if he doesn't want them?" Kim asked.

"I don't care what he wants," Avery murmured. But she did care; she cared that he didn't seem to want her.

Kim chuckled. "When you mentioned this special feature before, you wanted to do it to thank and acknowledge Dawson for saving your nephews," she said. "Now I think you want to do it out of revenge."

Avery had a lot of reasons for wanting to do the feature: revealing the real story of the fire and finding out more about Dawson. The man fascinated and irritated her more than she cared to admit.

"Instead of telling him where to find you, I should have warned him to stay away from you," Kim murmured as she gathered up the breakfast stuff. "The man is in trouble now…"

"You're in trouble," Cody called out in a singsong voice as he joined Dawson in the gym.

Ignoring him, Dawson continued to pump the weight bar up and down. Up and down. His body ached, but not because he'd been working out for over an hour. It ached because he'd denied it the pleasure he knew he could have found with Avery.

He'd wanted her so damn bad. He still wanted her. For once he understood that edginess other guys got—like Superintendent Zimmer when he instinctively knew a big fire was coming. And Cody when he'd been in one spot for too long.

Dawson had that edginess now—it cramped his stomach muscles and tightened his groin. Unlike the other guys, his edginess had a name. Avery Kincaid.

"Aren't you going to ask why you're in trouble?" Cody asked.

He knew why. He was letting a woman get to him. Worse yet, a reporter. He just rolled his aching shoulders in a shrug.

"The boss is looking for you," Cody said. "He's expecting an update."

"Update?" Dawson was not in charge of finding out about the hot spots. Braden had taken on that responsibility himself.

"About the reporter," Cody reminded him.

He probably should have talked to Zimmer before now, told him about the ashes in the hearth and the eerie feeling of being watched.

But he wasn't certain what any of it meant. If Avery had already been talking to the arsonist, would she have been so unnerved? Or was it because she'd been talking to him and knew how dangerous he was that she'd been scared?

He had no idea. And sneaking out of her place just after dawn wasn't going to help him learn anything. Kissing her instead of questioning her wasn't going to get her to talk—not that she could with his tongue down her throat. The only thing he'd managed to get her to do was moan. But that hadn't been enough.

Would she have screamed his name as he thrust inside her? How the hell had he managed to leave her when he'd never wanted anyone more?

Sure, he'd been trying to do the right thing—the honorable thing. He'd only spent the night at her place to protect her. Because she'd been scared. Taking advantage of her fear and vulnerability would have made him a jerk. He was only supposed to find out if she knew anything about the arsonist, not sleep with her.

The blond firefighter stood over him—maybe to spot him as he continued to lift the weight bar. But he studied Dawson through narrowed eyes. "I stopped by your place last night," he said, "but you weren't home."

"No, I wasn't."

Cody's eyes narrowed more. "But you're always home."

Dawson snorted. "Nobody on the team is always home." Even Wyatt, who was crazy in love with his hot little redhead. "We're either on a fire, here, or at the Filling Station."

"It was late," Cody said. "You're always home when it's late."

Like the exercise and the diet, sleep was an essential part of their job, too. When they were out battling a blaze, they didn't get much of it. So on their downtime they had to catch up.

He hadn't gotten much sleep last night, though.

"So where were you?" Cody asked.

"Hopefully out doing his job," Braden Zimmer said as he joined them in the weight room.

"There wasn't a fire call last night," Dawson said.

"He meant the reporter," Cody said. "You should have been doing her."

He should have been. He wished like hell that he had—because he suspected she wasn't going to give him another opportunity. She was too proud and too angry with him. Hell, he might never see her again. He should have been relieved; the last thing he wanted was a reporter hounding him the way they used to. But instead of relaxing, his stomach muscles tightened more.

"He should have been *talking* to her," Zimmer said.

"I thought the point was to get her talking," Dawson said. Because he had no intention of talking to any reporter—especially not Avery.

"Did you get *her* talking?" Braden asked.

"I questioned her as much as I could without making her suspicious," he replied. Knowing she already was, he amended, "*More* suspicious."

Zimmer cursed. "You think she knows about the arson?"

He shrugged. "I don't know what she knows." She'd answered his questions, but she could have been lying about having no other sources than the twins. She wouldn't want to reveal who she got her information from; she was a reporter after all.

So she could have been lying to him. He'd been pre-occupied—first with making sure she was safe. And then he'd just been preoccupied with her—with wanting her.

He wanted her so much that it was almost as if he could smell her—the light flowery fragrance that was completely out of place in the firehouse's sweaty work-out room. He could feel her, too—her closeness—as his skin began to tingle.

And then he heard the unmistakable click of heels against the concrete floor of the hall. And his body began to tense.

It couldn't be...

8

AVERY WINCED AT the echo of her heels against the concrete. Maybe she should have worn more sensible shoes. But she'd needed her armor of high heels and a silk dress that hugged her body. Looking professional reminded her that she was just a reporter doing her job. And Dawson Hess was just a story. Not a man who had recently rejected her…

The rejection wouldn't have bothered her if she wasn't so damn attracted to him. Her focus was usually on the next story, the next step in her career, the next move. Not a man with whom she could have no possible future.

She stopped just outside the last room on the left where that curly-haired kid had directed her to. No one must have yelled at him about talking to her, because he had been as helpful as ever when he'd told her they were in the workout room. Then he'd told her where to find that room.

Only a few of them were inside, he'd said. Superintendent Zimmer, Cody Mallehan and Assistant Superintendent Dawson Hess. Dawson had never said he was an assistant superintendent.

But then, he'd never said much about himself.

She'd gone to the wrong source for the information she wanted. She'd tried to investigate but the US Forest Service provided very little information about their Hotshots. There was no list of names or who held what position available to the public. If not for Superintendent Zimmer talking at the press conference during the fire, she probably wouldn't have known he was in charge. And of course Dawson had told her nothing the night before. He was the only male she'd met who didn't like talking about himself. So she would talk to the others about him. She would get his story whether he liked it or not.

She drew in a deep, bracing breath. She *could* do this; she *would* do this. It was good she'd dressed professionally because it reminded her that she was a reporter. And a reporter's face was a blank slate. She couldn't betray any bias, or any reaction at all to what was going on around her.

So her eyes didn't drop out of her head and her tongue didn't roll across the floor like some cartoon cat who'd found a juicy bird spinning on a rotisserie when she walked into the room.

Dawson Hess wasn't spinning. But he was lifting. His shirt off, every muscle in his chest rippled as he effortlessly—almost absentmindedly—lifted the barbell in his hands. Sweat trickled down between his pecs and rolled across his washboard abs before disappearing into the waistband of his low-slung shorts.

The man was as hot as the fires he fought. He was also oblivious to how damn sexy he was. And to her…

He remained focused on his workout while his co-workers turned to her.

"Good morning, Ms. Kincaid," the superintendent greeted her. His coolness from the day before was gone; he seemed almost friendly.

Why?

She narrowed her eyes. She'd expected more rejection. When she'd tracked them down at the little tavern, they had all been adamant that they didn't want any more media attention.

"Good morning," she replied.

The morning was almost gone, though. She'd wasted too much time worrying about what to wear; she'd told herself that she was only doing it for herself—so that she'd feel professional. But she realized now that she'd wanted Dawson's reaction.

Instead, she got Cody Mallehan's. The blond firefighter was openly staring at her. His green-eyed gaze ran up and down her legs. She hadn't thought Dawson was paying attention until she saw him bump Cody with the end of his barbell.

Cody grunted and glanced down at him. "What? That weight getting too heavy for you, old man? Want me to show you how it's done?"

Dawson bumped him again. Then he effortlessly lifted and snapped the barbell into the holders at the top of the bench.

Avery knew how strong he was from how easily he'd lifted and carried her to her bedroom. But now she saw the muscles bulging in his arms and in his broad shoulders. She closed her lips to hold in a wistful sigh at the sight of the sweat glistening on his skin. Then she dragged her gaze from Dawson's impressive physique back to his friend, who was pulling off his shirt.

"I'd actually like to ask you some questions," she told the blond firefighter, "if you have time."

Cody paused and glanced at his boss. She didn't notice anything, but Superintendent Zimmer must have given him an imperceptible nod, because the guy began to speak, "So you finally found out Wyatt Andrews wasn't the only hero the day of the big fire."

And her gaze returned to Dawson. He'd tensed.

"I know he wasn't," she said. "Dawson rescued my nephews."

"The twin blond kids?" Cody asked.

She nodded. "Kade and Ian Pritchard."

"Cute kids," Cody said. "Hess did take care of them. I was there, too, though. Hess and I went back together to find Wyatt and the campers."

Mallehan was the kind of man she was used to—the kind who wanted his accomplishments noted.

"Wyatt found them first," Dawson said. "He got them clearing ground to set up the fire break. He was the true hero."

Cody sighed. "Yeah, he was."

"But Dawson brought the extra shelters," Cody said. "He made sure there were enough for everyone."

Dawson shook his head. "There's no point in dredging all this up again," he said. "It happened several weeks ago."

"But the true story was never told," Avery persisted.

When the men all exchanged furtive glances, she knew her instincts about the fire hadn't failed her. There was even more to that story than Dawson Hess's heroism. And she vowed to find out what.

DAWSON SHONE HIS flashlight beam around the ground, looking for footprints in the soft soil beneath the trees in the yard of Avery Kincaid's little cottage. He should have looked the night before, but he hadn't wanted to leave her alone in the house. He should have looked that morning, but he'd known then that if he didn't walk back to her sister's place, get in his truck and drive off, he would go back inside. And he would make love to her.

Idiot...

That was what his body had been calling him the entire day. The intensity of his workout hadn't eased any of his tension. He ached with it—ached with wanting her.

And it hadn't helped that she'd showed up at the firehouse in mile-high heels and a skintight dress. The gold silk had nearly been the same color as her skin, making it all too easy for him to imagine her in nothing at all.

Cody had obviously been imagining her naked, too. He'd followed her around the firehouse like a puppy while she'd talked to the other members of his crew.

Why had Zimmer allowed it? They'd been determined to avoid drawing more media attention to the fire. What the hell did he think a special feature was going to do?

Sure, the guys had been careful to say nothing about how the fire had started. But she'd asked, and she had to have noticed that no one had actually answered her. They'd asked her questions, too, but she'd been just as careful and hadn't revealed any of her suspicions. And Dawson knew that at the very least she suspected something. Maybe she even knew that it had been arson; maybe that was why she was being so persistent. She wanted to be the first to break the news.

The arsonist would love that—would love finally getting the attention he wanted. Whoever set the fire must have been the one inside Avery's place—the one who'd been watching her. The beam of light bounced across the ground. It had been disturbed. The imprints were large, the tread deep. The boots belonged to someone bigger and heavier than her nephews—just as he'd suspected when he'd heard the branch snap the night before. Someone had been out there, hiding in the trees and watching her.

He strode back to his truck. He needed to call Superintendent Zimmer and let him know what he'd found—what he suspected. But what could Zimmer do? If he sent anyone to check out the area, she'd know for certain that there was more to the story. That was why Dawson had waited until night to investigate, in the hopes that she wouldn't notice his looking around her yard.

He tossed his flashlight inside and leaned in to reach across the console to the passenger's seat. Something hard dug into his lower back. He'd parked near trees. He'd had no choice since the driveway was barely wide enough for his truck. But none of those trees had low-hanging branches. It had to be something else.

Someone else…

"What the hell are you doing?" Avery asked.

"What the hell were you doing today?" he asked. And instead of reaching across the seat, he reached behind him and wrapped his hand around the oar as he turned to face her. He didn't jerk it from her hands; he pulled slowly enough that she came with the oar and fell against him. Her hips pressed into his—only the narrow wooden part of the oar separated her breasts from his chest.

"What do mean?" she asked. And she sounded breathless. "What was I doing?"

"Coming down to the firehouse," he said. "Talking to my friends."

All proud and professional, she lifted her chin and haughtily replied, "I was doing my job."

"You're still determined to do this special feature on me?" he asked.

She nodded.

He shook his head. "You're wasting your time."

"It's my time to waste."

"Isn't it your station's time you're wasting?" he asked.

He couldn't believe a major-market news program would care about a fire that had happened weeks ago.

"I took a week off from the station," she said. "So it's my time."

A week. That was all she was going to be in Northern Lakes? He could last a week surely—hold off her questions that long. Hold off his desire for her…

Maybe her questions, at least…

And he might not even be in Northern Lakes a week. Hopefully he and the rest of the Huron Hotshots would be called to work another fire, far away from her.

"It's your time," he agreed. "But it's my life. If you want to know about me, talk to me—not to my friends."

Because he was afraid they would say too much, give up enough details that she could actually run something about him. Unfortunately they had confirmed that he'd been the one to rescue her nephews. Damn Cody's big mouth. He didn't need or want to be in the media spotlight again. But she'd have to dig deep to find out about his past. He just wanted to do his job—and part of that job was stopping the arsonist.

She snorted. "Like you're going to tell me anything…"

He chuckled. They hadn't known each other long, but they were getting to know each other well.

"What were you doing?" she asked. "Shining a flashlight around my yard?" The dome light in his truck cast a glow in the yard—over her face, which was pale. He'd scared her.

He shouldn't have risked shining the light around, shouldn't have risked her noticing.

"My job," he said.

She glanced around. "I don't see a fire."

Not yet.

"I was checking to see if there were any footprints

around your yard, any indication that someone had been sneaking around here like you thought last night."

She cocked her head and studied him skeptically. "How is that your job?" she asked. "You're a fireman— not a police officer."

That was true. But in a small area like Northern Lakes, firefighters often pulled double duty. He worked as a paramedic in the off season, when the Hotshot crews weren't needed to battle major blazes.

"I was checking to see if you needed to call a police officer," he said.

"Do I?" she asked.

He shook his head. Then he released the oar. She stumbled back slightly with it. He turned and reached into his passenger seat for what he'd been trying to retrieve before she'd shoved the oar into his back. Pulling out his pillow, he said, "You don't need to call the police because I'm spending the night again."

She chuckled now. Bitterly. "Like hell you are."

"You're not safe being here alone," he said—especially not now that he'd seen those footprints. And if the arsonist had been there once, he could come back. Dawson didn't want to be there just to protect her; he wanted to be there to catch the fire starter.

"You just said I didn't need to call the police," she reminded him.

"Because you have me." He wished the words back the minute he said them—because it felt like that, as if she had him. Despite his best efforts to resist his attraction to her, she had him.

"You're a fireman," she said. "Not a bodyguard."

"I can protect you." Probably better than a bodyguard, since the person he suspected represented the threat to her safety was an arsonist. He just wasn't sure who could protect him from her.

"I don't need protection."

"You are pretty sure that someone was in your place last night," he reminded her.

She shook her head. "I talked to my sister. She doesn't remember cleaning the fireplace. Those ashes could have been there for a while."

He doubted it. Whatever had been burned hadn't been there long before he'd discovered it. "And the feeling that someone was watching you?"

"Paranoia?"

He could have showed her the footprints—could have proven to her that her instincts had been correct. "Maybe you're right," he agreed. "But what if you're not? What if someone had been inside—what if he comes back? You can't take the chance of being alone."

She snorted. "I don't take unnecessary risks," she said. "I had dead bolts installed today. And I'm keeping my can of Mace close."

He chuckled. "I guess I'm lucky you didn't bring that out here."

"I recognized your truck," she admitted.

"So you didn't want to Mace me," he said. "Just whap me with the oar."

"You deserved to get whapped with the oar for sneaking around out here in the dark," she said. "I wanted to save the Mace in case there's a real threat."

Then with the prickly pride and stubborn independence he was beginning to find strangely endearing, she lifted her chin and said, "I'm perfectly safe."

Not from him. He'd spent the day cursing himself for not having sex with her. And his body had punished him for denying it the release it needed. Maybe he'd only looked for those footprints to give himself a reason to stay.

Now he had to give her a reason to want him to stay—to want him…

Tossing the pillow back into his truck, he reached out and wrapped his hand around the oar. Then he pulled it and her back toward him—as if he was reeling her in. She stumbled on the uneven ground and fell against him again.

Her beautiful turquoise eyes widened with surprise. Maybe she felt it—the hardness of his body, his erection straining against the fly of his jeans. "Dawson…?"

"You're not safe," he said. "You're not safe at all…" And he lowered his head to hers.

9

AVERY HAD NEVER been more afraid. Her fear had nothing to do with a potential stalker and everything to do with Dawson. Just as with every other time he'd kissed her, her knees weakened and her body quivered. Since she'd come outside in the cool night air, she'd been cold. Heat flashed through her now, and she no longer noticed the chill. She was unaware of everything but his lips on hers.

His hands were on the oar; he wasn't touching her anywhere but her lips. His mouth slid over hers—gently back and forth. But then he increased the pressure, and her lips parted on a gasp of desire. His tongue slipped inside her mouth, driving deep.

And her desire increased. She wanted that tongue on other parts of her body—wanted him inside her. And she wanted to touch him, too. So she tightened her grip on the oar. She didn't want to reach for him only to be rejected again.

That was why she was afraid. She had never wanted anyone as much as she wanted this man. But she worried that she might want something she couldn't have.

Sure, he seemed to like kissing her. He'd done it often

enough, but then he always walked away. Just like those other times, he lifted his head from hers and stepped back.

Regret formed a hard knot low in her stomach—where she ached for him. He turned away back toward the open door of his truck.

Summoning her pride, she forced herself to say, "Goodbye."

But the driver's door slammed—with him outside the truck. He turned back to her and, his voice gruff, said, "I told you I'm spending the night."

"And I told you I don't need protection." She didn't want him to stay because of the thing his friends had dubbed his hero complex. She'd spent some time at the firehouse—trying to get them all to talk about him. But they'd been reticent—especially with him staring at them threateningly. The teenager who washed their bright yellow trucks and cleaned up the firehouse had told her the most—as he usually did. He'd told her that all the Huron Hotshots talked about Assistant Superintendent Hess's hero complex. Whether it was from fires or bar brawls, he couldn't stop himself from stepping in and saving people. She intended to use that for her special feature, but not for herself.

"We both need protection," he said.

"Why?" Was he in danger, too? The firefighters in Detroit had been in danger; those gang members had threatened them, too. As if fighting fires wasn't dangerous enough, they'd had to worry about bullets and knives, as well. What the hell had really caused the fire in Northern Lakes? She intended to find out, even if her life was threatened again. She was a reporter, so it was her job to uncover the truth.

He reached out and grabbed the oar. "You won't need this anymore," he said, as he tossed it into the bed of his pickup truck. Then he reached out and grabbed her. His hands wrapped around her waist, he lifted and slung her over his shoulder, fireman-style.

"What the hell are you doing?" she asked—as she already had once that night. And she wriggled around, trying to slide down.

He held her with just one hand on the back of one of her thighs. She felt the imprint and heat of his palm through the thin material of her yoga pants.

"Have you lost your mind?"

His deep voice still gruff, he murmured, "Probably..."

She dangled down his back as he carried her toward the cottage. She'd left the door open, light spilling out. He walked over the threshold and kicked the door closed.

She pressed her hands against his back and tried to push herself up so she could slide over his mammoth shoulder. But the hand not on her thigh touched her butt, easily holding her in place.

Her skin tingled and heat coursed through her, along with desire. He kept walking—across her living room— to her bedroom door. He'd carried her there the night before, but unlike last night he kicked the bedroom door closed with them both on the inside.

Finally, his hands moved back to her waist and he pulled her from his shoulder. Her body slid over his, down the tense, rigid length of him.

Her breath shuddered out on a gasp as desire overwhelmed her.

His chest rose and fell, pushing against the thin material of his black T-shirt, as if he was breathing hard, too. But she'd watched him effortlessly lift a barbell that weighed far more than she did. He hadn't physically exerted himself.

She stared up at him. For once she was incapable of asking all the questions burning inside her.

But he answered her anyway. "We both need *protection*," he said. "Because I'm staying the night and I'm not sleeping on the couch again."

She had to clear her throat before she could reply. "I told you it's the most uncomfortable couch I ever owned."

"It's uncomfortable," he agreed. "Just like I've been all day…"

"You hated having me ask questions about you."

"You made me uncomfortable," he said. "But you did that yesterday." He reached for her hand and pressed it to the fly of jeans. "You made me uncomfortable because you did this to me. You made me want you…"

"You want me?" But he had rejected her.

"I've been miserable since last night."

She had been, too—even more so after seeing him shirtless and sweaty in the firehouse gym. He'd looked so sexy. She stroked her fingers over the hard ridge of his cock beneath the denim. "I don't want you to be miserable."

Her hand trembling slightly, she fumbled with the button on his jeans—freeing it before she slid down the zipper and released him. His cock pushed out the thin material of his boxers, tenting them toward her.

She reached for it, but he caught her hand in his. And a groan slipped through his lips. "It's going to be over too quickly if you touch me," he warned.

"I want to touch you," she said. "I want to taste you…"

He groaned again. "I do need protection," he said. "Not just for you but from you. You're dangerous…"

She giggled at the thought of his feeling threatened by her. "Me?"

"I know you're ambitious."

"Why is that a bad thing?" she asked. "I want to be successful." She wanted airtime, and respect for being a good reporter, not just a pretty one.

"It's not a bad thing," he said. "As long as you don't use other people to achieve your goals."

"You think I'm using you?" she asked. And now she tensed. "You don't think very much of me if you believe that."

"I think you're beautiful and smart and determined."

"I am determined," she agreed. "And I want to find out the whole story about the fire."

He tensed now, and his amber eyes burned as he stared down at her. "So you do just want the story."

Her pride be damned, she admitted, "I want you."

His hand still on her wrist, he pulled her forward—into his arms. He lowered his head, kissing her passionately—his tongue sliding in and out of her mouth.

She lifted her arms to slide them around his shoulders. But he pulled back.

Had he changed his mind?

She held her breath, waiting to see what he would do. His hands moved to her waist. He tugged up the knit material of her loose sweater and pulled it over her head. Her hair tangled around her face. But before she could push it back, his fingers were there—sliding through the strands.

"Your hair is so silky," he murmured. Then his fingers trailed down her throat, over her collarbone to the curve of one of her breasts.

She wasn't wearing a bra, hadn't felt as though she needed one beneath the loose sweater. But then she hadn't been expecting anyone to show up at her house—least of all Dawson. He had looked beyond irritated at the firehouse earlier.

But maybe that had been because he'd been as tense and achy as she'd been all day—achy with wanting.

"Your skin is so soft," he said, his voice going hoarse with desire. He skimmed his fingers around each mound, caressing every inch. Her breasts swelled and her nipples tightened.

A moan slipped through her lips. She needed him to touch her. As if he'd read her mind, his hands moved to her nipples. He brushed his thumbs across them, making them even tighter. And desire coursed through her—from the tips of her breasts to her core.

Heat and moisture pooled between her legs. That ache inside her intensified. She needed him there.

He lowered his head. And his lips moved across her breasts before closing over a nipple. He tugged on it gently before nipping it lightly with his teeth.

She cried out—not because he'd hurt her. But because he'd made her come—just a little. Not enough to ease the tension she'd built inside her.

He tensed and asked, "Are you okay?"

She shook her head.

"Was it too hard?"

"Not hard enough," she said. "I want you." Want wasn't adequate to describe how she really felt, though. It was more than want. It bordered on desperation.

He lowered his head again and scraped his teeth over the point of her nipple. The sensation was both torture and ecstasy. She tunneled her fingers in his soft hair and clasped his head against her breast. He continued the torment—moving his mouth from one breast to the other.

And drove her out of her mind…

"Please," she implored him as she pulled at his shirt. He stepped back and dragged it off. The muscles in his arms and chest bulged and rippled. Then he kicked off his boots and dropped his jeans to the floor.

She reached out for his boxers. She wanted them off, too, wanted to see every sexy inch of him. He was male perfection.

But he stepped back, eluding her touch. "Not yet," he murmured, his voice so gruff she could barely understand him. "You first."

She reached for the waist of her yoga pants. But he lifted her and laid her on the bed. Then he peeled the pants down her hips and legs and dropped them to the floor.

His breath escaped in a rush. "You're not wearing panties."

The yoga pants had them built in, but she didn't explain that to him. She didn't have time before he was touching her. He ran his hands down her legs, his palms gliding along the outside of her thighs and calves.

"They go on for miles," he murmured. Then he wrapped his fingers around her ankles and tugged her down, so her butt was at the end of the mattress. His hands slid back up her legs—to her knees—which he pushed apart.

Was he going to make love to her like that? Him standing up and her lying down? She didn't care how he wanted to do it—just that he did.

But he didn't shuck off his boxers. Instead, he dropped to his knees. She felt the soft brush of his hair against the inside of her thigh, then the heat of his breath.

Anticipation coiled with the tension inside her. She didn't have to wait long for the brush of his lips. His tongue flicked out, teasing her clit, which already pulsed with desire.

Then he used his hands, too. One reached up for her

breast, cupping it, before he slid his thumb across the nipple. The fingers of his other hand stroked over her before sliding inside.

She arched up, pushing against his mouth and his hand as little spasms began to move through her body from her nipples down to her core. He sucked at her clit now as he drove his fingers deeper inside her. She shuddered as the spasms intensified to an orgasm so overwhelming she screamed his name.

HIS NAME ECHOED inside the bedroom. He'd known she was passionate just from her little moans the first time he'd kissed her. He'd had no idea the intensity of that passion until he tasted it. She was sweet—like honey.

He wanted to feel it, too. Hands shaking slightly, he pushed down his boxers. Then he reached for his jeans and pulled out a condom. Before he could tear it open, she took it from his hand.

Had she changed her mind?

He tensed, waiting for her to send him away. But she said nothing. She just slid off her bed and dropped to her knees in front of him. Staring up at him with those gorgeous turquoise eyes, she watched his face as she closed her lips over the tip of his cock.

He groaned at the sensation—at her tongue moving around the end of him. She lapped at the drop of desire that slipped from him. Her mouth was small and tight. She couldn't take much more than his tip inside it. But she parted her lips and sucked him deeper.

She was driving him crazy with her mouth. And her fingers moved at the same time, stroking over his sensitive skin.

His groan turned into a growl. A warning. He was

going to come. But he didn't want to come like this. He pulled away from her. "I have to be inside you."

He had to feel her—had to drive as deep as he could. Her fingers trembled as she fumbled with the condom packet, so she ripped it open with her teeth. Then she rolled it down the length of him.

"You're so big," she murmured. "I should have known you would be…"

He lifted her from the floor—lifted her into his arms. She clasped his shoulders then slid her hands over his biceps. "You're so big everywhere…"

He was big. And, swollen with desire, he might be too big for her. He laid her down on the bed, and she parted her legs and arched—ready for him to thrust inside.

He nudged the tip of his cock into her slick opening. She was so hot—so wet. Knowing she was ready, he slid deep. Her inner muscles gripped him, tugging him deeper yet.

She lifted her legs and wrapped them around his hips. As he thrust down, she moved up—matching his rhythm. Her breasts pushed against his chest, the nipples still tight. Her hands moved over his back, her nails scraping the skin. And her mouth touched him, too, sliding over his shoulder.

He moved his head, so that he could kiss her. And as he drove inside of her, he moved his tongue between her lips. In and out.

Her tongue tangled with his. She sucked at it—the same way she'd sucked his cock. He'd already been aching with desire before that. Now his body was so tense— his erection throbbing and pulsing—that he could barely hold back.

But he wanted to give her another orgasm. He moved his hands to her legs. Unlocking them from behind his waist, he lifted them. They were so long that they stretched beyond his head, and were so damn silky against his chest. He leaned into her—driving deeper than he had been. He reached between them and pressed on her clit, rubbing his thumb over it.

Her hands clutched his back and she moved against him—increasing the pace of his thrusts as she lifted her butt. She bucked beneath him, seeking her release. He felt it come over her—felt the contraction of her muscles, then the hot rush as the orgasm flowed through her. She screamed his name again.

He drove harder—not for her now, but for him. As her muscles continued to contract, squeezing his cock, his tension finally broke. His body shuddered with the intensity of the orgasm as he came. A shout slipped through his lips.

He collapsed on his side, pulling her to him as he recovered, tucking her head against his shoulder.

After a few minutes, he rose to discard the condom and clean up. When he came back to the bed, she had pulled up a blanket and snuggled beneath it.

Apparently she hadn't gotten any more sleep than he had the night before, because she was out, her lips slightly parted as she breathed deep and easy. He wanted to slide beneath that blanket and wrap his arms around her.

But she'd been right earlier. She didn't need his protection. She had the dead bolts. Mace. He had no reason to stay. Except longing…

He wanted to make love to her again. But he was already getting too involved. He'd thought having sex with her might cool the heat of the attraction between them. But it had only made it hotter.

He couldn't risk staying—couldn't risk getting in any deeper with her. He was a simple guy. An honest guy.

When he was with a woman, he had no secrets. If she questioned him then, he would be tempted to tell her everything. And the Hotshots would be furious if she ran a story about the arson. Worse yet, the arsonist might thrive on that attention and start more fires. He couldn't risk it—couldn't risk her getting to him any more than she already had.

He grabbed his clothes and hurriedly dressed. But desire for her had him stopping at the bedroom door. He turned back. The blanket was thin, doing nothing to conceal the curves of her body. He wanted her again—wanted to peel back that blanket and cover her with himself instead.

Would she be mad that he left? Or worse yet, hurt? Or would she be relieved?

She couldn't actually want a relationship with a guy like him—a guy based out of sleepy Northern Lakes, the town she couldn't wait to leave as a kid. She'd only been back as much as she had because of the fire, because she knew there was more to the story.

No. He'd be smart to run as far and fast as he could from Avery Kincaid. She was dangerous—because she was a reporter and because she was getting to him. Yet he couldn't make himself move toward the door. He couldn't leave her.

But then a sound pealed out from his cell. It wasn't a phone call; it was the siren that called him back to the station—to a fire.

He jerked open the bedroom door and hurried out, hoping it hadn't awakened her. He didn't need to worry about her. She would be safe.

If it was another arson, the arsonist wasn't likely to go far from the fire he'd set. He would be as drawn to it as Dawson was drawn to Avery Kincaid.

10

AVERY FLINCHED AT the piercing sound of the siren. While she wasn't really on vacation, she had promised herself no alarm clocks at the beach house. So she reached out sleepily, slapping the top of the bedside table to shut it off. But there was nothing on the table but the wrapper from the condom she'd rolled onto Dawson Hess's long...

She jerked fully awake.

Dawson. Where was he?

The bed was empty but for her and the tangled sheets. The siren was gone, too, replaced by the sound of a closing door and then a truck engine. He was leaving.

Because of his alarm? But that hadn't been an ordinary cell phone alarm. It had sounded more like a fire alarm.

He'd left for a fire. Maybe she should have felt better— that he hadn't slipped out after making love with her because that was all he'd wanted from her. Sex.

Incredible sex. Mind-blowing sex. She'd never felt anything as intense as the pleasure he'd given her. He'd instinctively known just where to touch her to drive her crazy. And when he'd used his clever tongue on her...

The orgasm had shattered her so completely that she hadn't thought she could have another. But he'd felt so good inside her—driving so deep. And when he'd touched her clit, she'd been helpless to do anything but come again.

The intensity of their passion had overwhelmed and exhausted her. She hadn't meant to doze off. But then she hadn't thought he'd slip away, either. He'd said that he was going to spend the night with her—in her bed.

Of course, if that siren had been for a fire, he'd had to leave. He'd had to do his job—his *real* job. He was a firefighter. Not a bodyguard. Not a police officer.

So what the hell had he been doing shining the flashlight around in the dark earlier? Why was he so concerned about whether or not someone had been inside her cottage?

Who did he imagine it could be?

She suspected he had someone in mind—someone other than a neighbor nosy about the renovations she'd had done to the place or a vacationer who'd forgotten which cottage they'd rented. Was that why he'd really come over? To shine that light around—or had he come to make love to her?

Despite just having had the most incredible sex ever, frustration built inside her again. Now that she knew how amazing it was between them, the desire she felt for him intensified. She was greedy for more of the pleasure he'd given her. Nerves joined the frustration inside her, fluttering like the wings of a hundred butterflies. She couldn't be getting attached to Dawson. Attracted was one thing…

But attached… She'd never let any relationship get that serious before. She'd always been too focused on her career. On a story…

And there was a story here in Northern Lakes, one she was pretty certain Dawson was trying to keep from her. But for the first time in her life she wanted more than the story.

She wanted the man.

DAWSON BRACED HIMSELF at the end of the hose, his arms burning as he directed the blast of water toward the last of the flames. Cody stood beside him, his feet planted hard in the scorched ground as he helped Dawson with the hose. Wyatt was on the other side of Cody while Zimmer was in the truck.

They'd only needed the four of them—the ones who worked out of Northern Lakes when they weren't out with the entire Hotshot crew. This fire hadn't called for more firefighters; it wasn't like the beast that had torn through the national forest so many weeks ago. It was just a small fire within the previously scorched part of the forest.

The flames dropped as the smoke grew—dark clouds rising into the dawn sky. They directed the hose, sending the blast of water over the ground again—making sure no hot spots fired back up.

It was only later, as they wound up the hose, that they spoke.

"You weren't home again last night," Cody remarked.

"Who the hell are you?" Dawson asked. "My mother?" But his mom hadn't talked to him for years, not since he'd joined the US Forest Service fire department—as his stepfather had so many years before. Her not talking to him hadn't been all bad, though. She was never going to put the past behind her; she enjoyed dwelling on the tragedy and wallowing in the sorrow too much. He'd had to move on, had to let it go so that it wouldn't consume him as it had her. But if the press—if Avery—dredged all that up again...

He could lose his peace of mind as well as the job he loved.

Cody snorted. "Like I would know how a mom acts..."

The younger firefighter had no family. He'd grown up in a series of foster homes. He claimed he'd liked being raised that way—that staying in one place for too long would have driven him crazy.

Dawson figured it mattered who was in that place with you. He sure as hell hadn't wanted to leave Avery. If the call hadn't come in, he would have given in to temptation. He would have crawled back into bed with her; he would have wound his arms around her and held her tight. But no matter how tightly he held her, he'd have to let her go. She didn't live in Northern Lakes; she was only here for a week. Less than a week now. Even less if she got her story sooner.

"Trust me," Dawson said. "You're acting like my mother." She'd always been so overprotective—always wanting to know where he was going and what he was doing. She'd tried to control his life so she wouldn't lose him. But in trying to control him, she'd lost him faster.

Cody shuddered. "Maybe it's good I never had one, then. I'd hate having to answer to anyone—which is another reason I don't want to ever get married."

Dawson chuckled at the hypocrisy of his friend's reply. "So, you don't want to answer to anyone, but you want me to answer to you?"

Cody chuckled at himself. "Hey, you're the one with the special assignment."

"Right now I'm just concerned about the fire," Dawson said. It was out but for the last puffs of smoke wafting from the burned ground, but he wanted to know what or who had caused it.

"What do you think this was?" Wyatt asked their boss.

Braden had been studying it, walking around the area. "It could be another hot spot," he said—almost reluctantly.

"You don't sound entirely convinced of that," Dawson observed. And neither was he. The ground had been so scorched from that first fire—everything so dead. What could have ignited it, let alone fueled it?

There shouldn't have been any hot spots. There was nothing left to get hot.

That wasn't the case at all with the fire that had burned between him and Avery. It had been hotter than any passion he'd felt before. Her heat and her desire had scorched him. But it hadn't burned itself out. Not yet. He'd intended to spend the night with her but not to sleep. He knew there was so much more to experience. So many ways they could bring each other pleasure. But when he'd found her sleeping, he'd had an anxious moment—feared that he was getting in too deep.

He'd already brushed that fear aside though when the siren had sounded. He'd intended to go back to her. To make love to her again.

And again.

Dawn had only just broken. She probably wasn't awake yet. He could go back to her—could crawl back into bed with her. Or he could have if he hadn't locked the door to keep her safe.

Of course, he hadn't been able to turn the dead bolt from the outside. But locking the door should keep out whoever had been inside the cottage the other night. The lock would also keep him out.

"What do you think?" Wyatt prodded their boss to reply.

Braden sighed. "It's been really sunny and dry. It could just be firing back up on its own."

"Could?" Cody asked.

Braden shrugged. "We'll do some more tests for accelerants—see if anything turns up here."

Dawson had an uneasy feeling that it would. Because if the arsonist was still in Northern Lakes, he wouldn't be able to resist setting another fire. The urge would be too great; he'd have to keep burning things.

Had he been the one who'd burned whatever had created the ashes in Avery's fireplace? The one whose footprints he'd found around the trees?

Why was he watching her? Because he'd already made contact with her or because he wanted to?

Dawson had to figure out some kind of test of his own—some way he could learn how much Avery really knew.

As if he'd read Dawson's mind, Braden asked, "What about you?"

"What about me?" he asked. He had his opinion about the fires, but until they had confirmation, he intended to keep it to himself—which was probably exactly why Braden was reluctant to offer a definite opinion. He didn't want to alarm anyone with news that the arsonist was still around, still preying on the town in which they lived, in which they had friends and family.

Sure, they cared about the blazes they battled in other states. They wanted to protect the people and the property. But it was different at home—it was more personal. Dawson had a feeling that it was for the arsonist, too. That was why he'd started the fire in the national forest, why he'd stayed here.

Because he probably lived here, too.

"Have you learned anything from the reporter?" Braden asked him.

Dawson had learned a lot but none of it had anything to do with the fire.

"What could he learn from me?" a familiar female voice asked.

It wasn't the question he'd expected her to ask. But then he hadn't expected her to show up here at all. He whirled around, alarmed to see her standing just outside the wafts of smoke. They had machines running yet. The fire engine. A backhoe. No wonder they hadn't heard her little Jeep or her approach. But he should have sensed she was near. "What the hell are you doing here?"

He flashed to all those times he'd had to rescue reporters who'd gotten too close to a fire. Too many times…

People like her—career driven and overly ambitious—needlessly endangered themselves and others. It annoyed him when other reporters did it; it infuriated him that she had. "You can't be this close to the fire."

She peered around him. "What fire? All I see is smoke."

"How'd you know where to find us?" Braden asked. He'd been nice to her the day before—too nice, in Dawson's opinion. That niceness was gone now. He didn't like reporters at the scene of a fire any more than Dawson did.

Despite the coldness of his boss's question, she smiled as if he'd wished her a good morning. "That curly-haired kid is so helpful."

More likely helpless to resist her charms. Dawson could hardly blame him, though, when he hadn't managed to resist her himself. While he hadn't told her anything about the fire or really about himself, he'd gone to bed with her. And he wanted to again—so badly that he might reveal things he had no intention of revealing…

Cody cursed. "That damn kid…" He'd been the one

to vouch for the teenager and get him the part-time job working at the firehouse. Like Cody, the kid had grown up in foster homes. Once Stanley had turned eighteen, he'd had to leave his last one and go out on his own.

Dawson suspected Cody had helped him out with more than just getting the job. And he teased Dawson about having a hero complex...

"What happened here?" she persisted as she gazed around at the smoke rising from the scorched earth.

With her sunny blond hair and golden skin, she looked so out of place in the middle of all the darkness. Everything that had once been just as beautiful and vibrant was gone now. And the hot spots firing back up hadn't allowed any of the vegetation to start growing again. It was as if the fire—or the arsonist—was determined to keep this area dead.

His voice gruff with fear for her safety, Dawson replied, "Nothing that concerns you."

"Sounds like it does," she said. Her turquoise eyes hardened with anger and suspicion, she focused on his face and asked, "What were you supposed to find out from me?"

Was that all she'd heard? What about Braden checking for signs of accelerants? Had she heard that too?

And what would she do with the information? Put herself in danger, no doubt.

Ignoring her question, he replied, "You can't be here." Dawson wrapped his arm around her waist and turned her back in the direction she'd come from.

She squirmed in his embrace. Just a short while ago, she'd clutched at him, her nails digging into his back, and struggled to get closer to him. Now she struggled to get away.

But he held her closely as he guided her over the black

ground to her older model Jeep Wrangler. He opened the driver's door for her. "It's not safe for you here."

Her face was flushed and he could see the anger in her eyes as she glared at him. She'd heard enough that she was mad at him, mad that he'd been trying to get information from her.

"The fire's out," she said.

He suspected she wasn't just talking about the flames they had extinguished. She wasn't going to let him spend the night again—not on the couch and most especially not in her bed.

11

"HE USED ME!" She had never been so furious. It didn't matter how many times she'd paced her sister's kitchen— her fury hadn't lessened. She nearly trembled with it.

Kim laughed.

"So much for being a sympathetic big sister," Avery griped. And she shot Kim a glare every bit as venomous as the one she'd given Dawson when he'd all but shoved her back into her Jeep at the fire scene.

Kim laughed again. "It's hard to be sympathetic when you had fully intended to use *him*."

Heat flushed Avery's face. It was probably from all the pacing. She wasn't embarrassed. Even if he had used her, she didn't regret having sex with him. She regretted more that they wouldn't be doing it again. "I wasn't using him!"

"You don't want to do a story about him?" Kim asked.

"Yes, I do," Avery said. "But that isn't using him."

"But he doesn't want you to do the story," Kim reminded her. "Are you sure the story is really what you want?"

"Yes," she said. There was definitely a story there. She would get it despite him. "That's all I want."

Kim smiled skeptically. "Sure it is."

"It is now."

"Oh," her sister said with a nod of realization. "You slept with him."

She hadn't *slept* with him. He'd slipped out while she'd been sleeping. Sure, he'd been called out to that fire. Her face heated again over how he'd rushed her away from that fire as if she had been just a pesky reporter to him, as if he hadn't seen her naked and been inside her...

"He acted all sweet and protective," Avery said. And she'd fallen for it, for that hero complex of his. But after what she'd heard, she didn't think he was a hero at all.

"But he was just using you for sex?" Kim asked.

"I don't think so," Avery admitted. He hadn't been with her for sex or because he'd wanted her; he'd been with her for information. And that was why she was so furious.

What had he been supposed to find out from her? She was still asking herself that a while later when she drove up to her cottage. She hadn't walked even the short distance between Kim's place and her cottage since the other night—since she'd had that eerie sensation of someone watching her.

Even though she'd rushed out after Dawson that morning, she'd been careful to lock the door. She was probably overreacting. Those ashes had probably been inside the fireplace already—the smoke smell just from one of the bonfires on the beach.

But she'd rather be safe than sorry. That was why she couldn't let Dawson distract her again—why she had to focus on the fire and not on the desire she felt for him.

Finding the door still locked, she breathed a sigh of relief as she turned the key in it. She didn't have to worry about anyone being inside now. But as she stepped over the threshold, her foot slipped and she nearly fell. She regained her balance and looked down to see what had tripped her. Someone had slid an envelope under the door.

Had Dawson left her an apology? It hardly seemed his style. But then she hadn't thought that using her was his style, either. So much for that hero complex everyone—including her—had thought he possessed...

She studied the envelope. The handwriting definitely didn't look the way she would have imagined his. The letters were big and loopy—almost childlike. And it had been addressed to Miss Kincaid instead of Avery.

No. The letter wasn't from Dawson. It was probably Northern Lakes's version of junk mail, some kid's offer to mow her lawn or something. So she didn't have a burning need to open it at the moment. Her burning need was to speak to Dawson, instead—to find out exactly what he had been expected to learn from her.

Heat pooled low, and that ache she'd had for him returned—the pressure building inside her. She had a burning need for him, too. Still...

Even though he had apparently just been using her. And he'd acted as if he was worried *she* was using *him*. She hadn't been. But she should.

She'd been watching her station online. Another new reporter had been hired. To replace her? Hopefully not. It had already been difficult enough to get airtime. Now it would be harder yet. Unless she broke a big story soon...

Hearing a vehicle drive up, she shoved the envelope into her purse. Then she glanced out the front window. Her heart rate quickened when she saw the black US Forest Service truck nearly scraping between the trees. Dawson had come to see her again. To use her?

Heat streaked through her, but it was the heat of desire more than anger. Maybe she wanted him to use her after all.

Moments later, her door vibrated from the force of his knock. She eagerly opened it with the playful threat, "I should whap you with the oar again."

She should have checked that it was him before she opened her door. Because it wasn't Dawson standing on her welcome mat.

"Again?" her visitor asked. "I don't believe you've ever whapped me with anything, Ms. Kincaid."

THE KNOCK AT his door didn't surprise Dawson. Apparently Cody had been coming by the past two nights. Dawson had thought it was just to razz him about his special assignment to get the "hot reporter" to talk. But maybe he had another reason. Maybe Cody wanted to talk himself.

He had an uneasy feeling Cody might want to talk about leaving. Dawson didn't want to lose a valuable team member and a good friend. But they'd all wondered how long Cody would stick around before the wanderlust got him. Sure, they traveled all the time for their job. But they'd been spending more time this season at their home base because of that damn arsonist.

Maybe it was too much—or actually not enough—for Cody. He wanted more action.

Dawson did, too. But the action he wanted had nothing to do with his job and everything to do with Avery Kincaid. He would have gone back to her place tonight—if he hadn't doubted she would let him in.

But when he opened his door, it wasn't Cody he found standing on his porch. It was her.

He sucked in a breath. Her turquoise eyes sparkled in the light spilling out of his cabin. God, she was beautiful. "How did you find me?"

Unlike Braden and Wyatt, who had places close to the firehouse, he and Cody were stationed out in the forest.

"I'm a reporter." She shoved past him to step inside his cabin. "I know how to track down a story."

He wasn't sure letting her inside was that smart. But the breeze was brisk, and his hair and skin were still damp from the shower he'd just taken. So he closed the door—shutting out the chill even as he shut her inside with him. "I'm not a story."

Not anymore. And he damn well wouldn't be again—not even for her.

"You should be," she said as she glanced around the place. There wasn't much to see. It was an open space with his bed in the middle. The kitchenette was off to one side, the door to the bathroom off the other wall. "Even your boss thinks so."

"What?" When Dawson had left the firehouse earlier that evening, Braden had mentioned that he was going to do damage control with the reporter. Making her more determined to do the special feature about him sounded more like damage expansion to him. More damage than Braden realized. "What did Zimmer tell you—besides where I live?"

What the hell had his boss been thinking, to let her know where to find him?

Oh, yeah, Zimmer wanted him to find out what she knew about the arsonist. At the moment Dawson was more worried about what she knew about him.

"Superintendent Zimmer said that he's worked with you for years," she replied.

Sometimes he forgot how long it had been. He'd joined the Forest Service fire department fresh out of college, and he'd requested to be assigned to this area even though he hadn't grown up here. He'd grown up out West. So it might have been easier for him to get hired onto a Hotshot team out there, especially if they'd known who he was. But he hadn't wanted anyone to know who he was.

Panic gripped him, tightening his stomach into knots. She couldn't know…

She couldn't find out.

Avery continued, "But he still doesn't know that much about you."

There was a reason for that. Dawson had worried that if Zimmer knew too much he might reassign him to another Hotshot crew. And he had his reasons for wanting to be on this team—with a particular team member.

"That's because there's not that much to know," he said. "There's nothing special about me for your feature."

"You've said that before," she said. "I didn't believe you then. And I don't believe you now."

Was that the only thing she didn't believe? She'd looked at him earlier as if he'd betrayed her, as if she couldn't trust him and wouldn't let him near her again.

She wasn't looking at him that way now. She was looking at him the way he always looked at her—with lust. Her gaze traveled down his chest. His shirt was in his hand instead of on his body. He hadn't even buttoned his jeans yet; they hung low on his hips.

As her gaze skimmed down there, his cock swelled and pressed against the zipper. "Avery?"

She looked up, and her face was flushed—with the same desire he felt for her.

"I thought you were mad at me," he said.

"I was."

"That's why I didn't come over tonight," he explained. But he'd wanted to—so badly—just like he wanted her.

"Superintendent Zimmer came by instead," she said.

And for a moment a strange feeling tightened his

stomach muscles into tight knots. Was that feeling jealousy? He didn't immediately recognize it because he'd never felt it before. He had never been serious enough about any other woman to be possessive of her.

But Avery Kincaid was the last woman he should feel that way about; she was only in Northern Lakes for a week. Then she would be returning to her big city job and big city life.

The thought should have given him relief—should have assured him that he was in no danger of getting too attached to her. She wouldn't interfere with his focus on his job any more than he would interfere with hers. But instead of feeling relieved, that knot tightened more in his guts.

"Why did Zimmer stop by?" he asked. Just what had damage control entailed? Not that he had any reason to be jealous of his boss. Everyone knew he was still hung up on his ex-wife—which was another good reason Dawson should be grateful Avery was leaving soon.

He didn't want to wind up as heartsick as Braden was over a woman. Nothing was worth the kind of pain that man had suffered.

"He wanted to explain what I'd overheard earlier," she said.

"What did you overhear?" Anything about the accelerants?

"He thought you had agreed to do the feature," she said. "And he was asking you if I'd told you when it was going to air."

What did you find out from the reporter?

Zimmer's explanation wasn't a big stretch. Except for one thing...

"Never," he said. "That's what I was about to tell him when you walked up."

YOUR PARTICIPATION IS REQUESTED!

Dear Reader,

Since you are a lover of our books – we would like to get to know you!

Inside you will find a short Reader's Survey. Sharing your answers with us will help our editorial staff understand who you are and what activities you enjoy.

To thank you for your participation, we would like to send you 2 books and 2 gifts – **ABSOLUTELY FREE!**

Enjoy your gifts with our appreciation,

Pam Powers

**SEE INSIDE
FOR READER'S
SURVEY**

For Your Reading Pleasure...

We'll send you 2 books and 2 gifts
ABSOLUTELY FREE
just for completing our Reader's Survey!

YOUR READER'S SURVEY
"THANK YOU" FREE GIFTS INCLUDE:
▶ **2 FREE books**
▶ **2 lovely surprise gifts**

PLEASE FILL IN THE CIRCLES COMPLETELY TO RESPOND

1) What type of fiction books do you enjoy reading? (Check all that apply)
○ Suspense/Thrillers ○ Action/Adventure ○ Modern-day Romances
○ Historical Romance ○ Humour ○ Paranormal Romance

2) What attracted you most to the last fiction book you purchased on impulse?
○ The Title ○ The Cover ○ The Author ○ The Story

3) What is usually the greatest influencer when you <u>plan</u> to buy a book?
○ Advertising ○ Referral ○ Book Review

4) How often do you access the internet?
○ Daily ○ Weekly ○ Monthly ○ Rarely or never.

5) How many NEW paperback fiction novels have you purchased in the past 3 months?
○ 0 - 2 ○ 3 - 6 ○ 7 or more

YES! I have completed the Reader's Survey. Please send me the 2 FREE books and 2 FREE gifts (gifts are worth about $10) for which I qualify. I understand that I am under no obligation to purchase any books, as explained on the back of this card.

150 HDL GJ2A/350 HDL GJ2C

FIRST NAME	LAST NAME

ADDRESS

APT.#	CITY

STATE/PROV.	ZIP/POSTAL CODE

READER SERVICE—Here's how it works:

▲ If offer card is missing write to: Reader Service, P.O. Box 1867, Buffalo, NY 14240-1867 or visit www.ReaderService.com ▲

BUSINESS REPLY MAIL
FIRST-CLASS MAIL   PERMIT NO. 717   BUFFALO, NY

POSTAGE WILL BE PAID BY ADDRESSEE

READER SERVICE
PO BOX 1867
BUFFALO NY 14240-9952

NO POSTAGE
NECESSARY
IF MAILED
IN THE
UNITED STATES

She smiled—a coy, sexy smile that had his muscles tightening in other places. His cock throbbed, demanding attention. Her attention...

"I'm not agreeing to it," he said. "I don't need any special attention for doing my job."

She stepped closer and reached out, trailing her fingers down his chest. "You don't need *any* special attention?"

"Avery..."

Her fingers dipped lower. Metal scraped as she lowered the zipper of his jeans. Then she pushed her hand inside the waistband of his boxers and her fingers slid around his erection.

He groaned as his control ebbed away. The intensity of his desire for her pushed aside his concern about her doing a special feature on him. At the moment nothing mattered but her—sliding deep inside the heat and the heart of her.

He scooped her up and carried her the few short steps to his bed. Then he dropped her gently onto it. She bounced on the soft mattress and giggled.

But he swallowed her next laugh as his mouth covered hers. He kissed her with all the passion burning inside him. He slid his mouth over hers before pressing hard enough to part her lips.

One of her sexy little moans slipped out—along with the tip of her warm tongue. She slid it across his bottom lip and then into his mouth. Their tongues tangled, sliding around each other. Her fingers reached for him again and slid around his cock at the same time, pumping it up and down.

He pulled back, tugging himself free of her seductive grasp. "Avery..."

She tensed as if she thought he might reject her—as if he could.

"You're overdressed," he observed. And he pulled off her sweater. Unlike last night, she wore a bra beneath it— some frothy lace concoction that did nothing to hide the color of her nipples or the tightness of them. He touched them through the lace, teasing them with his thumbs.

She moaned again and squirmed on the mattress. He wanted to build the same tension in her body that she'd built in his. So he continued to tease her nipples.

But she touched his chest, sliding her palms over it before she grasped his shoulders and urged him back down on top of her. But he had other ideas…

He pulled back and dragged off her jeans, taking the wispy lace of a G-string down her legs with the denim. Then he stroked his fingers over her core.

She squirmed some more and cried out. "Dawson…"

He looked up at her flushed face. Her eyes were wide with surprise. "You…" she murmured hoarsely. "You drive me crazy…"

"At least it's mutual…"

She grasped his shoulders, but he was too heavy for her to move. He pulled back and dropped his jeans and boxers. He found a condom in the table beside his bed and sheathed his cock. He didn't trust himself to let her touch him again. He'd probably come right away. And he wanted this to last.

Hopefully there was no damn fire tonight.

When he settled onto the bed beside her, she pushed at him. But she didn't shove him away; she only shoved him onto his back. Then she straddled his hips and lowered herself onto his shaft.

"Avery…" Her name escaped him in a groan. "You feel incredible."

Her inner muscles tightened, pulling him deep inside her. She rose up, then lowered herself again.

He reached for her. First he tangled his fingers in her silky blond hair and pulled her head down for a kiss. Then he moved his hands down her shoulders to cup her breasts. As she rode him, he stroked her breasts and teased her tight nipples with his thumbs.

She gasped, and her muscles tightened even more as she began to come. He clutched her hips then, increasing the pace to a frantic rhythm.

She shuddered and screamed her pleasure.

He loved the sound of it—loved how she nearly sobbed it as her body shook. He continued to clutch her hips, continued to drive the rhythm—until she bit her lip.

"Dawson…" His name slipped out again as if she couldn't help it.

Then she began to move frantically. The tension must have wound inside her once more. His cock was pulsing—desperate for the release. He needed it like he needed air.

Like he needed her…

But he wanted to drive her as crazy as she drove him. Then she tensed and shuddered as she came again.

He couldn't stop thrusting his hips up—thrusting inside her. And he came with an intensity he'd never felt before—not even the previous evening with her.

How was it that it got hotter between them?

Was their attraction like the big fire—too powerful to ever stop burning?

12

COMPLETELY SATIATED FROM the most incredible night of sex she'd ever experienced, Avery stretched like a cat. She felt like purring. Actually, she felt like making love again. She reached out, but her hand encountered only the wide expanse of empty mattress. Dawson was gone. The sheets had even cooled. He'd been gone awhile.

Had he been called to another fire? She hadn't heard that siren ring out from his phone again. But then, she'd been beyond exhausted when she'd fallen asleep. She might have slept through it.

She uttered a soft sigh of disappointment. She wasn't just upset that he was gone. She was upset with herself. Despite all her pep talks that she could handle her attraction to him—that she wouldn't lose her focus again—she hadn't asked him a single question beyond "Does that feel good?" and "Do you like that?"

Even those questions he hadn't really answered—with anything beyond a guttural groan of satisfaction. He had to have been as satiated as she was.

She felt boneless. She knew she needed to get up. He'd let her sleep but he hadn't really invited her to stay. She actually couldn't believe that he'd left a reporter alone in his house. But just as he didn't talk about himself, he was probably careful to leave nothing around that would reveal anything about him.

She forced herself to get up and dressed. And she looked around—with only a slight pang of guilt over invading his privacy.

The cabin was sparsely furnished. The bed dominated the room. Then there was a small table near the kitchenette. It had only two chairs pulled up to it. And in the opposite corner there was a short sofa and a TV.

Nothing hung from the log walls. No pictures. No awards. She sighed. The house was as elusive as its resident. She returned her focus to the bed. And her face flushed as she remembered all the things they'd done to each other in that bed—leaning over that bed, leaning off that bed…

Dawson didn't need to verbally express himself when he made love as thoroughly and passionately as he did. The man was as incredible a lover as he was a firefighting hero.

She couldn't include that in her special feature about him, though, and not just because it would be unprofessional and a betrayal of his trust. If word got out about what an amazing lover he was, Dawson would have even more women after him than the usual firefighter groupies. And Hotshots—being the most elite team of firefighters—had more groupies than most to start with. When she'd covered the Northern Lakes fire, she'd seen all those women. They'd looked almost as desperate as the parents worried about their missing children.

But unlike the parents, who'd looked as if they hadn't slept or eaten in days, those women had looked as if they'd stepped out of a salon. Their hair had been more expertly styled than Avery's when she had to be on camera—their makeup even more elaborate.

Another pang struck her, but this one wasn't guilt; it was jealousy. She didn't want those women throwing themselves at him. But they undoubtedly already had. After all, he was the best-looking man on the entire team. And they would continue to do so after she returned to Chicago. That was why she hadn't wanted to get involved with him—because she knew they had no hope for a relationship. But there had been no denying the attraction burning between them.

That was all it was, though—attraction. She wasn't developing any deeper feelings for him. Sure, he was the most heroic man she'd ever met. And sexiest...

But she didn't need a man. She wasn't ready to settle down—as Kim had—in Northern Lakes. And she didn't have that many days left of her week off before she had to return to Chicago. But she couldn't go back without a story. Or she might not have a job to return to.

She needed a very *special* special feature. So she ignored her pang of guilt over snooping and scrutinized the small cabin, trying to determine where something could be hidden.

She noticed again how high the bed was. Tugging back the blankets, she discovered why. Drawers were beneath it—a double set on both sides. The pang returning to one of guilt, she pulled open a drawer. In most of them she found jeans and T-shirts, underwear, socks...

It was in the last drawer that she found the personal stuff he hid away. Diplomas. One from high school. Another from college. He had a bachelor's degree in forestry studies from Michigan Tech. Instead of proudly displaying it, though, he kept it shut away. There were books, too. Thrillers. A couple of science fiction novels. There was also a leather binder. Her hands shook slightly as she pulled it out. This was it. A journal. A scrapbook. The history of Dawson Hess. Even before she flipped open the cover, she was certain of it.

But the picture inside that cover was old and yellowed, from a newspaper article two decades ago. Dawson would have been a kid then. Not the Hotshot hero who died trying to save a honeymooning couple—as the newspaper headline proclaimed. Martin Spedoske was the firefighter who'd died twenty years ago. So he wasn't Dawson's father. With light-colored hair and dark eyes, he looked nothing like the man Dawson had become.

Who was he that Dawson would have kept a scrapbook of him? There were several articles—all covering the same tragedy. The couple—who'd actually been on their second honeymoon—had been in a cabin in the middle of the forest a wildfire had consumed.

Martin Spedoske had found them, but not in time to save them or himself. He'd died in the fire. And so had Kevin and Susan Andrews.

While covering the story of Wyatt Andrews rescuing the lost campers, several reporters had brought up how he'd lost his own parents in a wildfire out West. Was it this fire? The one Martin Spedoske had also died in? It had to be same tragedy.

But why did *Dawson* have the scrapbook? It would make more sense that Wyatt Andrews would have it. The articles were old, so they were faded and difficult to read. She needed to go online and look up the original coverage of the tragedy to find out more. But when she picked up her purse and retrieved her phone, she found the screen ominously blank.

The weak cell signal up north always drained her battery. She dug deeper for her charger. She usually carried that with her. But she'd been in such a hurry to see him that she must have forgotten it.

She couldn't take the scrapbook with her. Snooping was bad enough. But stealing? She'd feel way too guilty if she did that. So she'd have to take notes the old-fashioned way—with a pen and paper. She found a pen in her purse, but she hadn't packed a pad. She usually took notes on her phone so she could put in reminders, too. There was only one piece of paper in her bag—the envelope she'd shoved inside last night. It didn't give her much room to write down all the dates and names from the articles. Maybe she could use the back of the letter—if the person hadn't written on both sides.

She tore open the envelope and pulled out the paper. There was only writing on the front—the message was short:

Miss Kincaid,
I thought you were a good reporter. How come you haven't figured out the fire was arson? The Huron Hotshots might be too cowardly to admit the truth, but I didn't think you were afraid of it. If you don't report what really happened, you should be scared—of what I'll do to you.

She reread the message. It could have been penned by a kook, by someone trying to claim responsibility for an act of nature. But she doubted it. Her instincts hadn't failed her. And she hadn't imagined that the Huron Hotshots had been trying to hide something from the public. Now she knew what it was: there was an arsonist jeopardizing the safety of everyone in Northern Lakes.

Anger coursed through her as she remembered her sister's terror and her own fear over the twins being in danger. She wasn't afraid of the arsonist or what he was threatening to do to her. She wasn't afraid of what she might do to Dawson for keeping the truth from her—for not making the public aware so that they could protect themselves.

No. She wasn't afraid at all. She was furious.

"THE ARSONIST IS definitely still in Northern Lakes," Superintendent Zimmer said, addressing the entire crew. He'd called all of his team to the meeting—even those stationed at firehouses in other areas of the country.

It had been hard leaving Avery—she'd looked so sweet and sexy curled up in his bed. But even if Zimmer hadn't said it, he'd known this meeting was important.

From the chair next to him, Cody turned and caught his gaze. When he'd heard that everyone had been called in, Cody had thought they were being flown out West to one of the fires still burning there. He'd been looking forward to going out to a big fire—to relieving some of the crews who'd been working them too long.

But Dawson knew what this meeting meant. If the arsonist was still in Northern Lakes, they had to stick close to home.

At least, it was home to Dawson.

What was it to Avery? Unlike him, she'd been born and raised in the village. But she'd left it years ago for college and she'd stayed away because of her career. She was unlikely to ever call it home again.

Not that it mattered. Not that he'd ever thought they could actually have a future. He wasn't a fool. He knew she was only been a reporter after a story.

The sex was just a bonus for her. He had no doubt that she'd enjoyed it. He had scratches on his back and his butt from her nails. And her screams of pleasure still echoed inside his head. Hearing them again, his body hardened, wanting hers.

Would she still be there when he returned?

He doubted it. What would she think when she awoke alone again? Would she be mad?

He should have left her a note. But what could he have said? Been called away to a top secret meeting? No. It was better that she hadn't been awake when he'd left. She would have known for certain something was going on in Northern Lakes.

They had confirmation now. But an eerie silence had fallen after Superintendent Zimmer's declaration. Everyone else might have been stunned, but Dawson wasn't. He'd known the arsonist was still in Northern Lakes. He suspected the man had been inside Avery's cottage, too.

"How do you know he's still here?" Ethan Sommerly asked. The guy was big and burly with an overgrown beard. When he wasn't with the team, he was stationed in the upper peninsula of Michigan—in a forest even bigger than the one where Dawson and Cody lived. But rumor was that he'd been raised in a big city—in a rich family.

Dawson never paid much attention to rumors, though. He didn't care where someone came from, just that they could do the job. And he trusted every one of the Hotshots on his crew to do their part—to have his back—during a fire or a bar fight.

Would they have his back when Avery learned the truth? She'd be furious with him when she did. And he had no doubt that she would eventually.

"The last two hot spots weren't random flare-ups from the original fire," Zimmer said. He spoke from a podium at the front of the big conference room on the firehouse's third floor. This was where they held their team meetings—and press conferences when they felt the public needed to be informed.

Avery would probably think they should have been. But Dawson understood why his boss was reluctant to do that. Zimmer didn't want to feed the arsonist's appetite for attention.

"The fires were deliberately set?" Wyatt Andrews asked. A muscle twitched along his tightly clenched jaw.

Zimmer nodded. He wore his tension in the tight lines around his mouth and the dark circles beneath his eyes. He'd obviously been losing sleep worrying about the fires—about the town. "Accelerant was found at both sites."

Dawson had been losing sleep, too, but not because he'd been worried. Guilt flashed through him. He'd let Avery get to him—he'd let her distract him. With an arsonist on the loose, he couldn't afford any distraction. Or any lost sleep…

They'd been given this break to protect their village and to catch up on their rest before getting called out to one of the big fires Cody was itching to fight.

He forced himself to forget about Avery—to forget the passion that burned so hotly between them. And he focused on the meeting.

"There had to be more than accelerant," Dawson said. There had been no vegetation left to burn.

"Bales of hay again," Zimmer confirmed.

"So it's definitely our guy," Cody said with a ragged sigh. "Sick bastard…"

"Do we have any information about him? Any leads?" another team member asked. Trent Miles worked out of a firehouse in one of the roughest parts of Detroit. He'd encountered more than his share of arsonists, but most of them were pros who burned down buildings for a percentage of the insurance money.

Their arsonist was different. He wasn't a professional. Burning down a forest had nothing to do with money. One of the other five motives for starting a fire was driving him: vandalism, excitement, revenge, crime concealment or extremism. They hadn't discovered that any other crime had been concealed, though, so that motive was unlikely.

"We're working on a lead," Cody said. Then he turned toward Dawson. "Have you learned anything from the hot reporter?"

Ethan Sommerly stared at Dawson, his dark eyes wide. "You're talking to a reporter?"

Ethan shared Dawson's aversion to the press. He probably would have found it easier to believe if Cody had claimed Dawson was talking to a unicorn.

"A hot reporter," Cody said, as if that justified it. "Avery Kincaid."

Trent Miles groaned. "She's a hot pain in the ass."

She'd worked for a Detroit station before. Obviously Miles had encountered her then.

"She's a hometown girl," Zimmer said. "If the arsonist contacted anyone in the media, it would be her. And she's in Northern Lakes this week." He stared out from the podium—his entire focus on Dawson. "So what do you think? Has he contacted her?"

The arsonist might have been the one watching her, the one who'd been inside her place. But Dawson didn't think she was aware of it.

He was reluctant to admit it—even to himself— because then he'd have no legitimate reason to keep seeing her. "I don't think she knows anything about the arsonist."

13

"IT WAS ARSON," Avery said.

Kim glanced up from the hearth. "It doesn't look like the fire did more than burn a single sheet of paper."

"Not that," Avery said. "I'm not sure what that was about."

A warning? The arsonist knew where she lived; he'd put the note under her door. Had he been inside that night she'd been so spooked? That had been the night she didn't lock her doors.

Had he burned the paper Dawson had found in the fireplace?

Kim shrugged. "It was probably just left from the last renters. I already told you that the weather was so warm I didn't think anyone would have started a fire."

And when Kim had told her that earlier, it had made sense because Avery had thought she'd been overreacting. But she wasn't overreacting now. The arsonist knew where she lived.

An arsonist didn't start a fire for warmth. He started it for pleasure. He got some kind of sick satisfaction from destroying things.

"But you always clean so well when the renters leave," she said.

Kim sighed. "I've been distracted since..."

"That fire," Avery said, and anger coursed through her again. Her sister had been terrified since that horrible day her children had been missing in the wildfire. "That's the one that was arson."

Kim tensed and turned away from the fireplace, almost as if she couldn't bear the sight of the ashes. "Someone deliberately set it?"

Avery nodded.

"Dawson Hess told you that?"

"Hell, no." Her anger intensified to fury that bubbled over again. He'd slept with her—more than once. But he hadn't shared anything with her—about himself or the fire. He'd just shared his body.

His incredibly hot, sexy body...

Heat flushed through Avery. But it was just anger. She was so pissed, yet strangely hurt, as well...

She'd let Dawson get to her in a way no man ever had before. She'd been drawn to his heroism, to how he'd protected her nephews. And she'd been even more attracted to his modesty over that act of heroism. He hadn't wanted any credit for it.

But it was more likely that he hadn't wanted any more attention drawn to the fire. He hadn't wanted the truth to come out.

Kim tilted her head and studied her. "Why do you think it was arson, then?" she asked. "There has never been any mention of it."

"Nobody's considered that it could have been?" Avery asked. She needed to learn more before she determined what to do about the note. She could turn it over to authorities. But...

Kim shook her head. But her face had tensed, lines pulling tight around her mouth. She looked older than thirty-two now. Those long hours worrying about her children had aged her.

"What?" Avery asked, and her concern was for her sister now—for how ill she suddenly looked. "What did you think caused the fire?"

Kim uttered a ragged sigh as she admitted, "Rick and I and the other parents kind of suspected that our campers might have inadvertently started it."

Avery gasped. "The kids? You think the kids caused the fire that nearly killed them?" She had always suspected there was more to the fire than the Hotshots had admitted. But she had never considered this possibility and she should have. Campers often caused fires.

Kim nodded. "The Scout leaders who took them on that trip were inexperienced. They probably didn't extinguish a campfire correctly."

And nearly cost themselves and the kids in their care their lives.

"But…" She had the letter. It was wrapped in plastic in her purse. She couldn't show it to Kim, though. If it was legit, she didn't want her sister involved—didn't want her threatened. Kim would try to protect her, and she had already been through too much. But Avery needed to show the letter to someone.

Dawson? If he'd been open and honest with her, she would have taken it to him immediately. But he hadn't been.

Superintendent Zimmer? She recalled the conversation the night he'd come to see her. He had claimed he'd thought Dawson had agreed to the feature. Knowing how adamantly against it Dawson was, she'd been confused at the time, but she'd just figured he'd been mistaken.

What if Zimmer had actually been playing her? What if Dawson had been playing her?

Did they suspect the arsonist might have contacted her? Were they trying to contain the story, keep it quiet?

If she turned over that letter to either one of them, she doubted she'd ever see it again. And without any evidence to substantiate her story, they could deny it. Hell, without any evidence to substantiate her story, her producer wouldn't even run it. No one would learn the truth.

"What makes you think it's arson?" Kim asked again.

"A source..."

"A credible source?" Kim asked. "When things like this happen, don't kooks generally try to claim responsibility?"

Avery sighed as she admitted, "Yes..."

The station routinely received calls and letters from people so desperate to get on the news that they claimed everything from alien abduction to organ harvesting had happened to them. Then there were the really disturbed ones who claimed to be serial killers or...

Arsonists.

She needed more evidence than that damn letter. She needed the fire marshal's report. It should have been a matter of public record. But Northern Lakes wasn't like big cities or even some of the counties. They had no on-line presence; no way to download or even order records. Northern Lakes didn't even have a police department—just a state police post. She'd stopped by and asked about the fire. But they'd told her that because the forest was national land, the US Forest Service had taken over the investigation.

Investigation? Was it routine? Or criminal?

"I would never run a story without confirmation," she

said. She'd never get it on the air. "I just don't know who I'd get to confirm it."

At the sound of a truck coming down the drive, Kim glanced out the front windows of the cottage and smiled. "You don't?"

Dawson shut off his truck and stepped from it, but he paused beside the driver's door. His handsome face was tense, his usually light eyes dark. Something was weighing on him—something he was too stubborn to share.

Frustration replaced her earlier fury with him. And as always, desire rushed over her. Why did he have this effect on her? "He won't talk."

Kim giggled. "So you two don't do much talking when he spends the night here? I assume you spent last night at his place."

"Kim…" Avery cautioned as he started toward the cottage, "don't say anything to him…"

"Getting shy, little sister?"

"Not about the sex," she said. "About the fire. Don't mention the arson thing to him."

"Maybe that's why you can't get him to talk," Kim said. "You're not talking, either."

Avery's face heated with embarrassment—over how she'd lost her focus. Every time she got around him she could think only about how much she wanted him.

Kim's eyes twinkled as she studied her face. "But then," she said, "sometimes you get farther without talking."

"What do you mean?" Avery asked.

She wriggled her eyebrows. "You get what Rick and I have."

Two kids and a house in the small town where she'd grown up? *No thanks,* she wanted to tell her sister. But she didn't want to insult her. Kim was happy with her life. Avery was the one who'd always wanted more.

As she stared through the window at Dawson Hess, she had to admit she wanted more—of him. But she wanted him to be the man she'd thought he was, the hero reluctant to take any credit for his selflessness. Not the man concealing secrets and seducing her into losing her focus on the story.

WHAT THE HELL was he doing here—again? Dawson asked himself. He no longer had an excuse to see her. She obviously didn't know anything about the arson. But he'd come back—because he hadn't been able to make himself stay away.

He was worried about her safety. She might not know anything about the arson, but that didn't mean the arsonist didn't know about her. Everyone in Northern Lakes knew about Avery Kincaid, about how smart and ambitious she was.

But those weren't the attributes that had attracted Dawson. It wasn't even her beauty. It was her obvious love for her nephews, her friendship with her sister…her determination to learn the truth.

She was beautiful, though. And sexy…

His body—his tense, aching body—had led him here. He had developed an addiction. To her.

She was only in Northern Lakes a few more days, though. He should have been relieved about that—that he would no longer be in danger of falling for her. But he had a sick feeling in the pit of his stomach. A fear that he was already falling. He lifted his hand to knock but the door opened before his knuckles touched the wood.

"Hello," Kim Pritchard said with a smile of amusement.

"Oh, I didn't realize…"

"That my sister isn't alone?" she teased. "I was just leaving." She brushed past him as she stepped outside. "It was nice to see you again, Dawson."

"You, too," he said. He turned as she started to walk away. "You're walking home?"

"——~ how I got here," she said. And her brow began to furrow.

"But it's getting late." It wasn't dark yet, but it would be soon.

"It's not far, as you know," she said. "And Northern Lakes is safe."

"Isn't it?" another voice asked.

He turned back to find Avery standing in her doorway, studying his face. She wore some impossibly short shorts—like tiny, nearly transparent boxers—and a tank top. He was glad the temperature hadn't dropped much tonight—just enough that her nipples had tightened into little buds that pressed against the tank top. He felt hot, though, his skin burning up from the heat of his attraction to her.

"Isn't it safe?" Avery asked again.

Her sister had stopped, too, and was staring at him.

He'd been an only child, but now he understood some of his friends' complaints about having sisters—about how they'd ganged up on them and skewered them with a look.

But it wasn't just the way they looked at him that made him uneasy. It was the question and how they'd asked it. As if they knew something they shouldn't—something he hadn't thought they knew.

"You thought someone might have been in your house the other night," he reminded Avery. "You installed dead bolts and started carrying Mace…"

Kim lifted her hand. "She gave me a canister of my

own." She glanced down at it. "I felt silly carrying it until…"

"Until what?" he asked. What did she know?

"Goodbye," Avery called to her sister. "You'll want to hurry home before the boys mess up your house too much."

"I *have* left them alone too long," Kim said.

But as she rushed off, Dawson didn't think it was her house she was worried about—it was her children. Either something had happened again or Avery had said something to unnerve her.

"What was that about?" he asked.

Avery moved her bare shoulders in a slight shrug. "She's been like that since the fire," she said. "Overprotective of her kids."

He nodded. "I don't blame her."

"She worries that something will happen to them again."

"Mothers sometimes worry too much," he agreed. His certainly had. She'd forced him into counseling so that he could talk about his feelings instead of dealing with them.

It wasn't until he'd become a Hotshot that he'd really dealt with them—by making his life worthwhile. He saved people.

But it wasn't possible to always save everyone. Just recently a Hotshot from another team had died in the fire out West. It had brought back memories, but he'd dealt with it.

"She has reason to worry," Avery said. There was that tone in her voice again, and her gaze was focused too intently on his face.

"Why?"

"Well, those hot spots keep flaring up," she said. "The whole town is in danger."

He shook his head. "We're monitoring the area closely. Nothing's going to happen again like that first fire." He stepped closer then, because he had to—because his body demanded contact with hers. His fingers brushed along her delicate jaw. "Your sister and her kids are safe."

She stared up at him, her eyes narrowed with skepticism. She knew more than she had when he'd left her this morning. Something had happened; she'd learned something…

"I'm sorry I had to leave this morning," he said.

"Was there another fire?"

He shook his head. "Just a team meeting."

"About the hot spots?"

Had she been hanging around the firehouse again? Had she overheard something? Cody's protégé had been on strict notice to not let her inside again.

"Just a team meeting," he repeated.

"You must have discussed something in this team meeting," she said.

"You…"

She lifted a hand to her chest—to her beautiful breasts straining against the confines of that tight tank top. She was killing him.

He felt sweat begin to trickle down between his shoulder blades. And it was finally growing cooler outside—where she'd left him.

"Why would you talk about me?"

"Trent Miles calls you a pain in the ass."

She grimaced. "That's one of the nicer things…"

Anger flashed through him. Had Trent insulted her? Sure, Dawson had lost his patience with reporters before. But Avery was different. Avery was…

Gorgeous. Sexy. Smart.

So smart that she was probably playing him—had

probably been playing him all along just to get information about the fire.

"He warned me to stay away from you." Before Dawson had left the firehouse, Trent had made a point of warning him about Avery. *She's so ambitious she's lucky she didn't get herself killed.* Since she'd been foolish enough to take on gang members, she'd have no qualms about trying to handle an arsonist. Maybe that was why Dawson had had to come to her—to make sure she was safe.

She shrugged. "I'm not surprised he would warn you."

"So why are you here?"

He couldn't use her safety as an excuse. She'd pointed out several times how she'd installed the dead bolts and started carrying her Mace around Northern Lakes. She also might begin to question why he thought she was in danger.

So maybe he was only distracting her. Or maybe he was giving in to the attraction he couldn't deny or control when he reached for her. He pulled her up tight against his body—so he could feel her breasts against his chest, her hips against thighs. And still it wasn't enough—not with clothes between them. He lowered his head and covered her mouth. It was the only way to stem her flow of questions. To kiss her...

He parted her lips and swept his tongue across the fullness of her bottom one. Then he nipped it lightly with his teeth.

She moaned and trembled slightly against him. So he lifted her in his arms. Then he kicked the door closed behind them as he headed for the bedroom.

He flopped her lightly onto the mattress. She stared up at him now—but there was no skepticism, no inquisition. Her eyes were dark with desire and confusion.

"How do you make my knees go weak?" she asked.

He leaned over to press a kiss against one of her sexy knees.

She shivered. "Dawson?"

His name was a question. One he had no problem answering as he trailed his fingers from her knee up her inner thigh. He dipped his fingers inside her shorts. She was already so hot—so wet. He dragged the shorts over her hips and down those long, sexy legs, while she pulled off her tank top. Her breasts sprang free, the nipples pointing right at him. He couldn't resist leaning forward and lightly nipping one.

She gasped—but that wasn't enough. He wanted to make her scream again as she came.

He sucked one nipple into his mouth while he teased the other with his thumb and forefinger—rolling it back and forth.

She squirmed beneath him as she pulled at his clothes—dragging his shirt up, unbuttoning his fly. She was as desperate for him as he was for her.

He stood up and finished undressing—except for the condom he rolled on. Then he joined her—joined with her—as he thrust inside her tight, wet heat. It felt amazing to be inside her, but he forced himself to pull out and enter her again, deeper this time.

"Dawson!" Her hands gripped his shoulders, her nails nipping into his skin. She leaned forward, pressing a kiss against the side of his neck, where his pulse pounded furiously. Her lips moved lower—down his chest. And she swiped her hot little tongue across one of his nipples.

The woman drove him out of his mind. And he intended to do the same to her. He reached between them and stroked his thumb over her clit.

She screamed now, the sound loud and intense as her body spasmed around him. She was coming...

A few more deep thrusts and he joined her, shouting her name.

"I'm not falling asleep tonight," she said, as if warning him. Or giving herself a pep talk. "We're going to actually talk."

He grinned. "Is that a challenge?"

"What do you mean?"

He wouldn't have thought it was possible, but he began to harden again inside her. If the only way to stop her questions was to make love to her, he'd have to make the sacrifice. He'd have to take one for the team...

14

SHE COULDN'T RUN a story without confirmation; her producer wouldn't allow it. And her personal ethics wouldn't, either. Dawson had given her nothing the night before—aside from hours upon hours of pleasure, of orgasms that had blown her mind and her body. She ached. Not just from what they'd done but because she wanted to do it again.

He was gone, though. Like the times before, he'd slipped away without a word. She'd awakened alone. But that had been hours ago.

She'd been working hard since then—working to get confirmation, to track down the story. The whole story.

"I'm Avery Kincaid from Channel Five out of Chicago," she said into her cell phone. She stood on her deck, where the reception was better. The lake shimmered in the sunlight.

Northern Lakes really was a beautiful area.

"Why are you calling me?" the woman asked on the other end. "Did I win something?"

From what Avery had read, it looked as if the woman had lost more than most—twenty years ago when her husband had died. "I'm calling about Martin Spedoske," she said.

"Don't you people ever let anything go?" the woman asked wearily. "He died so long ago..." Her voice cracked with emotion, though, as if the pain was still fresh.

"I'm sorry," Avery said sincerely. She couldn't relate to the woman's loss. But she remembered how scared she'd been when the boys had been trapped in the fire.

"I should have known..." Mrs. Spedoske murmured "...that it would all get dredged up again because of *him*." There was such bitterness in her voice.

Over the years of her career, Avery had learned that was how some people handled loss or tragedy—or sometimes any adversity. With bitterness. They never got over the anger stage of grief. She could relate. She had been angry when the boys had been in the fire. If it had been deliberately set, she would be even angrier.

"Him?" she asked.

"My son."

She'd found the woman's name in the dead Hotshot's obituary, but there'd been no mention of his having a child. "Who is your son?"

"Dawson Hess, of course," she replied. "I thought that was why you were calling—to ask about Dawson."

Avery's heart lurched as she realized this woman wasn't the only one who'd suffered a loss. Dawson had, too. That was why he'd kept the scrapbook, why he'd memorialized a dead man. Her heart ached for the pain he'd endured as a kid. Was that a pain from which you ever recovered, though?

"Yes, I am calling about Dawson," Avery said. "I just needed to confirm the facts. Martin Spedoske was his stepfather?"

"And his idol."

That explained why he'd kept the scrapbook—probably even why he'd become a Hotshot himself. He'd wanted to be a hero, like the hero he'd lost.

She couldn't imagine how his mother felt about his following in the footsteps of the husband she'd buried, though. Feeling the woman's pain, Avery remarked, "It must have been hard for you when your son became a firefighter, too."

The woman sighed again, raggedly. "That was when I stopped talking to him," she said. "And I won't..."

A pang struck Avery's heart—a pang of sympathy for Dawson. His mother had disowned him over his career choice, over his desire to save lives. He wouldn't have become a Hotshot—wouldn't willingly have taken on such a risky occupation—if he wasn't passionate about it. If it wasn't everything to him...

"I can understand that you'd worry, but..." Wasn't Mrs. Spedoske being harsh? Her son needed her support. Her love.

Her parents had always expressed their love for her and their pride. And all she did was report about heroes; she wasn't one herself.

The woman laughed but that, too, sounded bitter. "You can understand, but he can't. He was there—when we lost Martin. He was there when the press wouldn't leave us alone. He knows what I went through, the years of therapy. I even put him in counseling. Not that he would talk to the counselor..."

Avery held in a snort. She wasn't surprised that Dawson had refused to talk. Every time she'd asked him a question the night before, he'd kissed her...somewhere.

Mrs. Spedoske continued, "Dawson doesn't care about what he's putting me through. I wanted him to become an accountant or engineer."

Either profession would have bored him out of his mind. "He doesn't care that he makes me worry all the time," she continued. "He doesn't care about my feelings. I don't think he ever did. He never understood why I had to talk to the press—how it keeps Martin alive for me. He refused to talk to the reporters. He refused to talk to the counselor."

Avery realized the woman had been through a lot, but so had Dawson. It sounded as if she cared only about her own pain, though, and not what her young son must have gone through. While she'd wallowed in what she'd lost, Dawson had moved forward alone, and he'd found a way to honor the man he'd idolized.

Another pang struck Avery's heart, but she wasn't sure what this one was. Could it be love? She'd never felt it before. She'd never had time for love before. She didn't have time now, either. She wasn't at the point in her life—in her career—where she could fall now. She was probably going to lose her job if she didn't come up with a big story.

She was attracted to Dawson. She appreciated what he'd done for her nephews. She enjoyed making love with him. But it couldn't be any more than that. They could never have a relationship. Their lives were too different.

"I am grateful to your son," Avery said. "If he hadn't become a Hotshot, I would have lost my nephews. He saved them from a fire some weeks ago."

"I thought it was that other firefighter—the one whose parents Martin died trying to save."

"Wyatt Andrews found them," she said. "But Dawson and another firefighter helped saved the kids and Wyatt."

The woman began to laugh—almost hysterically. "So that's why you're calling, Miss Kincaid from Channel

Five in Chicago. There's your story, huh? How Martin couldn't save the parents but his stepson saved the boy?"

Avery tensed as realization dawned. It was actually a great story—one every reporter would have covered had they known the facts. But Dawson didn't want anyone knowing the facts.

His aversion to reporters had no doubt started when his mother had forced him to talk to them because she'd wanted the attention. Maybe that was why he was so willing to give Wyatt all the credit for the rescue.

Avery wasn't willing to let Dawson's heroism go without acknowledgment. Even if she didn't need a good story to get airtime, she would have run this one. Maybe Dawson would change his mind about reporters when he saw how she handled the story about him. He wouldn't be the victim of the tragedy that he had been twenty years ago. He would be the hero.

Her hero…

FRUSTRATION GNAWED AT DAWSON. He didn't want to be here. He wanted to be with Avery. She would only be in town a couple more days. And he wanted to make certain she stayed safe. The only way to do that was to stay with her.

But he was wedged into the back booth at the Filling Station, Cody on one side and Braden on the other. Wyatt sat across from them with Fiona beside him. Her brother, Matt, sat on the other side of her.

"Didn't think you'd be looking for an excuse to buy more beer," Zimmer remarked to Wyatt, who filled his boss's mug from the pitcher on the table.

Dawson held his hand over his mug. He didn't need any more beer. He needed Avery.

Cody held his mug out for Wyatt to fill. "What is the excuse?" he asked.

Fiona's brother held up a mug. But Wyatt skipped over it. The kid was big, but he wasn't twenty-one yet. Dawson was kind of surprised he'd joined them. After getting turned down for a firefighting job with the US Forest Service, Dawson had figured he'd be bitter. But he seemed happy with his decision to go back to school. Everything had worked out for the best.

Matt grinned when his sister smacked his shoulder. And Dawson noticed the glitter of a diamond on her left hand. He knew what the occasion was even before Wyatt announced, "We're engaged."

Cody shook his head. "That's a terrible mistake."

Wyatt sputtered out some curse words as his face flushed with anger.

And Cody laughed. "Not you. That's probably the smartest thing you've done. Fiona, you're making a terrible mistake. Why do you keep choosing this schmuck over me? He can't even find his way out of the woods alone."

She laughed. "Like you would ever propose..."

Cody sighed. "True. I'm not the marrying kind. So I guess I can understand your settling for the schmuck. Of course, that doesn't mean we can't have a hot affair."

Wyatt sputtered out some more insults, but he was grinning now.

"Congratulations," Braden said.

And Dawson wondered how much that cost him. Their engagement probably reminded him of how recently his ex had remarried. He had to be bitter. The whole team was—for him.

Dawson studied his friend's grinning face. Wyatt looked like a man confident in the love of a good woman.

Fiona O'Brien was an incredible woman. Beautiful. Smart. Empathetic. She understood why they'd chosen to be Hotshots—why it was important for them to help people. That hadn't always been the case, though. She hadn't been thrilled when her brother had applied, and she was probably hugely relieved his application had been rejected.

"Congratulations," Dawson said sincerely. He was happy for his friends—even as he knew he'd probably never find that happiness himself. Avery Kincaid wasn't the kind of woman looking for a ring or even a serious relationship. She only wanted a story.

Maybe it was good that he wasn't with her, because every time he was it was harder to leave her. He had been attracted; now he was getting attached. Maybe he was even beginning to fall for her…

"What's the occasion?" a familiar voice asked.

He glanced up to find Avery standing at the end of their booth. She was wearing one of her tight dresses—this one was a blue that nearly matched her eyes.

Cody whistled. And Dawson reacted instinctively with an elbow to his friend's ribs. Cody yowled.

"You never learn," Wyatt said with a pitying head shake, "to stop chasing after other guys' women."

They thought Avery was his woman? That was ridiculous. She wasn't the kind to belong to anyone but herself. Yet the idea gave him a momentary flash of pride and possessiveness. He'd never felt possessive before. Or jealous.

He'd never felt a lot of things he now felt for Avery, though. His stomach lurched as fear overwhelmed him. Maybe he wasn't just beginning to fall. Maybe he already had.

"We're celebrating our engagement," Fiona said, her face glowing.

Dawson shook his head. "You shouldn't have told her. It'll be all over the news now." He said it as if he was teasing—even though he really wasn't.

Avery must have realized that because she glared at him. "I don't report everything I hear," she said. "Not unless I can substantiate it…"

His stomach knotted at her ominous tone. What had she heard? What was she looking to substantiate?

Wyatt held up his fiancée's hand. "There's your substantiation," he said. "I wouldn't mind the world knowing this amazing woman agreed to become my wife."

"When's the wedding?" Avery asked.

"Not until the off-season," Wyatt replied. "I want to make sure we have a long honeymoon."

Fiona giggled, then blushed when her brother groaned in embarrassment.

"Don't put that in your report," Matt implored her. "What are you doing in Northern Lakes? A follow-up on the fire?"

Even though he hadn't introduced them, everyone knew who Avery Kincaid was. Her face was famous. Her body was incredible. Dawson shifted in the tight confines of the booth.

She gazed at Dawson, her stare as skewering as it had been the night before—before he'd distracted her with kisses and caresses…

He wanted to make that sacrifice again. But he was trapped in the damn booth.

"I have a couple of ideas," she said. "A couple different angles I can cover."

"Thought it'd be old news by now," Fiona said. "Nothing's happened in weeks."

"The hot spots—" Matt began.

"Are nothing unusual," Dawson interrupted him. "That happens all the time." When the fire hadn't been completely extinguished. They had completely extinguished it.

"Really?" she asked. "It's been so many weeks since the fire started that you'd think it would be completely out by now."

It had been completely out days after it had started.

"What makes you say that, Ms. Kincaid?" Braden asked. "Have you been researching fires?"

"Not fires in general," she replied.

Just one in particular, Dawson thought. "This isn't an interview," he told her. "This is an engagement celebration."

"You're welcome to join us," Fiona said.

Avery opened her mouth, but before she could either accept or decline the invitation, sirens pealed out from four cell phones.

Wyatt cursed. "Sweetheart, I'm so sorry—"

Fiona cut off his apology with a kiss. "Go."

Braden and Cody rushed out of the booth, sweeping Dawson along with them. He hesitated briefly next to Avery. He didn't expect a kiss. But he wanted one.

She stared up at him, her gaze focused on his mouth—as if she was considering giving him one. But Cody had his arm, dragging him along toward the door.

"We've got something hotter to fight than your reporter," he said. "And I think Trent might be right. She could be more trouble than even you can handle."

Too bad he hadn't realized that until it was too late. Until he was already in too deep with her...

15

AVERY'S HAND TREMBLED as she reached for the doorknob. She wasn't afraid someone had walked in; she knew she had locked it. Her fear concerned the fire to which the Hotshots had just been called.

Was it another arson fire?

Or just another of the mysterious hot spots?

She cared less about the actual fire, though, and more about the fact that Dawson was out there fighting it. She knew that was his job—and he was good at it or her nephews wouldn't be here. But still…

It was a dangerous job. Just a few weeks before, a Hotshot had died out West when the fire had jumped and consumed him and the pickup he'd been driving. That could have been Dawson; they'd been out West this wildfire season. They had battled that very same blaze.

The sound of an engine drew her attention away from her door. She glanced down her driveway. No lights shone. Nobody had turned off the street. It wouldn't have been him, anyway.

They couldn't have put out the fire that quickly. And they would have stuck around—would have made sure it was completely out.

As they'd done with the first forest fire.

So how did it keep reigniting?

She had researched fires, just as the superintendent had realized. But there was another subject that kept drawing more of her interest: Dawson.

She'd learned so much about him—so much of what made him the hero he was. The hero the world deserved to know about...

She unlocked the dead bolt. As she opened the door, it pushed a piece of paper across the hardwood floor.

Had another note been shoved under her door?

She should have been excited—hopeful that this would lead to the story she'd thought she would uncover in Northern Lakes. But irritation had a ragged sigh escaping her lips as she leaned down to pick it up. She had uncovered a story in Northern Lakes—one she had substantiated with that phone interview with Dawson's mother. With what his friends had admitted he'd done the day of the fire...

But Dawson didn't want her to run a story about him. She wanted to respect his wishes, but she didn't think he would be upset with her, with how she handled it. She would make everyone see how amazing he was.

How could he be upset about that?

And she would have an incredible story to present to her producer. One she was able to substantiate.

Her note-sender was probably just some kook trying to claim responsibility for something even her sister considered an accident. She only had a few days left before she returned to Chicago, so she didn't have time to investigate the arson claim the way she would need to. Given the amount of airtime the new reporter was getting, she couldn't even wait until she returned to present her producer with Dawson's story.

She had to give it to him now. So he would remember she worked for the station, too, that she was the special features reporter. She had worked on Dawson's story all afternoon. She carried the note over to the dining table where she'd left her laptop. Before she reached for the computer, she flipped the note open.

This one was even shorter than the last:

Miss Kincaid,
You're going to regret it if you don't share the truth with the public.

She shivered at the ominous message. Was he threatening her personally? Or the public in general?

He had called the Hotshots cowards. But who was the real coward? If he wanted her to tell his story, he needed to share more of it with her. But she was beginning to suspect he didn't have a story to tell—not a true one, anyway. Her sister thought the campers had started the fire, and that seemed more likely than an arsonist in Northern Lakes. And if it had been an arson, surely the Hotshots would have let the public know. They were heroes, after all. So maybe they were keeping the cause quiet in order to protect the campers who'd already been through too much.

At least Avery wouldn't leave Northern Lakes empty-handed. Clicking a button on the computer, she began to roll the footage she'd taped at the local television station—local as in a couple of hours away from Northern Lakes. Northern Lakes was too small to have their own television station. The footage was mostly her talking, sharing the story of Dawson's heroism and the reason he'd become a Hotshot in the first place.

Her heart swelled with pride in the man that he was—

the man she'd begun to fall for. He deserved to be acknowledged for what he'd done, for who he was.

She had some editing to do, but not much, before she sent the file off to the newsroom producer. She wasn't sure when or if he'd run it. If he ran it, how angry would Dawson be?

Would he understand why she'd done it? That it hadn't been to hurt him. She wasn't doing it just to help her career. But she suspected that it would. There was something compelling about the piece—about the man—that would resonate with the public.

Knuckles brushed softly against her door. The knock was too light to be Dawson or even Kim. "Who is it?" she asked.

"Fiona O'Brien," a female voice replied. "We met earlier tonight."

"The bride," Avery said as she opened the door.

"Not yet," Fiona replied. "The fiancée."

Avery narrowed her eyes in surprise. "Aren't you sure you'll make it to the altar?" They had seemed so in love. But then, what did Avery know about love?

The redhead's face appeared even paler than it had in the tavern. "You never know when you're marrying a Hotshot. The guy who died a few weeks ago," Fiona said, "he had a fiancée."

Avery stepped back. "I'm sorry. Please come in."

"I thought you had company," the redhead said. "I heard someone talking." Her gaze went to the laptop sitting on the dining room table.

And Avery suspected that Fiona knew who'd been talking and even what had been said. The cottage was strictly for summer use—the walls weren't insulated and the windows were single pane. If Fiona O'Brien had been standing outside the door for a while, she could have heard the entire special feature.

"Just me," Avery replied. The engagement ring on Fiona's finger made her part of the story now, so Avery hit the Play button.

On the computer monitor she sat in front of a green screen, so the production manager could put in whatever background he wanted. She spoke into the camera, "During this season we hear a lot about the wildfires raging in different parts of the country. But we hear less about the brave people who fight those fires—unless there's a tragedy. Then we hear only the bad. We need to focus more on the living heroes…"

She was totally focused on one particular hero. But she mentioned Wyatt and had included footage of him from the fire. And she mentioned Cody Mallehan—she thought he, at least, would appreciate being included. When she'd gone through the footage from the fire, she'd found images of him and Dawson arriving with the campers. She'd interviewed her nephews, who had loved being included. They'd gushed about how Dawson had rescued them and calmed their fears.

When the recording ended, Fiona released a shaky breath. "That was thorough." Tears glistened in her eyes as she turned away from the computer to look at Avery. "I didn't realize how close you and Dawson are."

"What do you mean?"

"The guys joke about how little Dawson says about himself. You seem to have gotten him to talk."

Heat flushed Avery's face. "I didn't have any input from him at all."

Fiona sucked in a breath. "He doesn't know you're doing this?"

"I told him that I was going to," Avery said. But he had no idea what she'd found out.

"But how did you find out so much?"

"I'm an investigative reporter," Avery explained. "It's what I do." And sometimes it could be almost as dangerous as fighting fires. So she'd try not to worry about Dawson. She knew how good he was at his job.

"You even talked to his mother," Fiona said, as if she was appalled.

Avery had been, too. "She's a piece of work. I can't imagine disowning her son because of his career choice."

Color rushed back into Fiona's face. "I can," she admitted. Then she hastened to add, "I wouldn't disown him or stop talking to him. But when my brother applied to the Forest Service fire department, I was scared to death. I didn't want him getting hurt."

Avery had covered too many tragedies. "People can get hurt anywhere," she said. The mall, the movies…bad things happened all the time.

"But for someone to purposely choose this profession…" Fiona shuddered.

And now Avery wondered if the other woman would actually make it to the altar.

"Someone purposely chooses this profession because they're a good person," she said defensively. Dawson had chosen the job to honor his stepfather, but also because he was a hero at heart. "And they want to protect other people."

"It's more than a job to them," Fiona admitted. "It's almost a calling."

Avery nodded. "It makes them who they are. And if you love someone, you love every part of them."

Fiona lifted her new diamond so that it twinkled in the

light. And she smiled. "I know." Then she turned toward Avery, and her smile widened. "You love him."

She tensed. "Who?"

"Dawson," Fiona said. "You love him."

"No—no," Avery stammered, and fear rushed over her again. She wasn't concerned for his safety this time, though. She was concerned for hers. "Absolutely not."

Fiona chuckled now. "You give yourself away in that special feature. You give away how much you care about him."

"I respect him," Avery said. "And I appreciate that he saved my nephews from the fire. And I want him to get the accolades he deserves."

"You love him," Fiona persisted. "And that's why I think you should erase that."

"What? You just said…" She couldn't repeat it because it might sound as if she was agreeing with Fiona. There was no way she sounded like a woman in love with her subject. She was a reporter; she'd been trained to never reveal her personal opinion of any story. No. Fiona was newly engaged. She was just seeing everything through the eyes of love.

"He'll hate it," Fiona said. "He'll hate being singled out. He'll hate even more having his past brought up again." She shook her head and red hair tumbled around her shoulders. "If you air that, you'll destroy any chance of having a future with him."

Avery snorted, albeit nervously. Would he be that furious? Surely he would understand. "We never had a chance of a future together."

It would never work. He was stationed out of Northern Lakes and she was just in Chicago until she found a position in a bigger market. New York. Or Los Angeles.

"Congratulations on your engagement and all," Avery

continued. "But I don't want that for myself. No marriage. No kids." She didn't want to settle down so young the way her sister had. She didn't want to be stuck in the town where she'd been born and raised.

"So maybe that's why you want to do this," Fiona mused. "To end it with him."

Avery shook her head. "There's nothing to end."

"I thought that too—a couple of months ago," Fiona said. "That it was just sex between me and Wyatt." She flashed the diamond at Avery. "It's not just sex."

"Obviously not between you two," Avery said. "But Dawson's never going to give me a ring." Not that she'd want one...

She was too busy. Too focused on her career. The last thing she wanted was a fiancé—or even worse, a husband. "No."

If she ran the feature, he would never give her a ring. But she doubted he would have anyway. Once she returned to Chicago, it would be over between them. Maybe it would be easier to end it like this—quickly.

Fiona opened her mouth but before she could say anything else, her phone chirped. She pulled it from her purse to study the screen, and a smile curved her lips. "They're fine. The fire's out."

"Another hot spot?" Avery asked.

"Nope, kitchen fire got a little out of control," Fiona replied. "Not too much damage—beyond the cook's bruised ego."

So it hadn't been a hot spot or arson. If there really was an arsonist in Northern Lakes, wouldn't he have started more fires? No, the story wasn't in the notes that had been shoved under her door. The story was Dawson Hess. That was why, when Fiona hurried off to meet her fiancé, Avery sent the video to her boss. She could have edited it more, but she hadn't wanted to risk chickening out because of the redhead's warning. Just how mad could Dawson get?

"I AM LOVING THIS," Cody said as he joined Dawson in the gym.

Dawson usually enjoyed a good workout, but he'd been punishing his body. Last night when he'd resisted going over to Avery's place, he'd denied his body the release it needed. Now he was lifting more weight, doing more reps than he probably should. He grunted and remarked, "You haven't even started yet."

"I'm not talking about working out," he said. "I'm talking about never having to buy beer again."

Despite the sweat dripping from his body, Dawson's blood chilled. "What are you talking about?"

Cody turned the tablet he'd been holding and pressed a button. Avery's beautiful face filled the small screen. Her eyes were luminous. Her lips so full and red and kissable. He loved the silky softness of them—loved how sweet her mouth tasted. Distracted by desire, it took him a moment to hear what she was saying.

Other images flashed across the screen. Footage from the fire. Twin boys telling about their fears and how he'd soothed them. Everybody in the damn video talked about him—about his life.

And *she* talked about his past. Something he'd never wanted dredged up again.

Betrayal hit him like a blow to the gut. She'd known how he felt about media attention, about reporters. And she'd ignored his wishes and run the story anyway.

"What the hell did she do?" But Cody wasn't the one he needed to ask. He threw down his towel. He didn't care how sweaty he was—he was going to skip the shower to confront her. If she hadn't already left…

"Hey," Zimmer said. "I need to see you in my office. Right now." He was definitely the boss today.

Cody cast Dawson a sympathetic glance as he followed Braden from the weight room. His office door was open—another man was already inside. Wyatt Andrews glanced up from the chair in front of Braden's desk and asked, "Did you deliberately seek me out?"

While Dawson didn't talk that much, when he spoke it was always the truth. "Yes."

Braden closed the door and settled into the chair behind his desk. The way both men stared at him now put Dawson on the defensive—because of her, because of what she'd done.

"It's not stalkerish and weird," he said. It was his damn mother and her endless bitterness. "For so many years I heard that my dad—stepdad—died for no reason. That it was such a waste."

Wyatt sucked in a breath. "He died trying to save my parents."

"Yeah. That was the kind of man Martin Spedoske was," Dawson said, in defense of the man he'd loved. "He hadn't cared that the risk was too great. He'd done everything within his power to save them—even giving up his own life."

"So you wanted to make sure that they were worth it," Wyatt said. "That *I* was worth his life."

Emotion choking him, Dawson couldn't speak. He could only nod. He couldn't even look at Wyatt—who was obviously struggling with emotions of his own—right now.

Why had Avery done this? Did she hate him?

She'd not only laid his life bare for the world to see and judge, she'd cost him a friend and probably his job. He turned toward his boss.

"Martin Spedoske definitely didn't die for nothing," Braden said, his voice gruff. As Dawson had, he'd also taken offense at what Mrs. Spedoske had said. "He gave me my two best Hotshots. If he hadn't died, I wouldn't have either of you on this team."

A pang struck Dawson's heart. It was true that he wouldn't have become a firefighter if his stepfather hadn't been one first. Wyatt nodded in silent agreement.

"Is it going to be a problem?" Dawson asked. "That we stay on the team together?"

Zimmer shook his head. "It's not a problem for me. We all have each other's backs—no matter what. No matter why. It's what we do."

"What about you?" Dawson asked. Did Wyatt think he was a stalker?

Wyatt shook his head. "Not a problem for me, either."

Dawson nodded. Then he opened the door to step back into the hall. He couldn't go see Avery now. His emotions were too raw. He wanted her to see only the anger, not all the other feelings she'd brought out in him. He headed back to the weight room where Cody had begun to pump the barbell.

Wyatt followed him into the room.

He braced himself. Wyatt might have held himself back in front of their boss. Maybe he intended to let him have it now.

"Say what you need to," Dawson invited him. He deserved whatever the other guy hurled at him. They'd worked together for years. He should have told Wyatt himself, before it came out like this. So publicly, thanks to Avery Kincaid.

How had she betrayed him like this? They'd made love. He'd begun to think they cared about each other. But she'd only been using him…

"Last night at the Filling Station," Wyatt began, "I couldn't ask you in front of Cody—"

"I'm right here," the blond firefighter interrupted from the weight bench.

Wyatt continued as if he hadn't spoken, "But I wanted to ask you to be my best man."

He sure as hell hadn't expected that. Had Wyatt really been going to ask last night? Or was he only asking now because he felt obligated.

"Really?" he asked. "Like Braden doesn't have that job." While Zimmer had been going through his divorce, he'd relied heavily on Wyatt. They were close.

Wyatt shook his head. "No, he doesn't. I want you."

"Why?" Dawson asked. "Because of that damn news report?"

"Because you're the one who saved my life."

"Yeah, still here," Cody murmured. "Was there, too. Is my name anywhere? In any of these reports?"

"Hey," Wyatt teased. "Just think of all the money you're saving. You don't have to buy drinks. You don't have to rent a tux…"

"Am I even going to be invited to the wedding?" Cody asked.

"Depends…"

"On what?"

"You going to hit on the bride?"

"Not at the wedding," Cody said. "That wouldn't be cool, even for me. I'll hit on Dawson's lady instead. He's going to be so busy with his best man duties—not losing the ring, doing the speech and all… You know how much he loves public speaking—he won't even notice."

But Dawson knew that wouldn't happen, because Avery Kincaid wasn't his lady and never would be. Not now. Not after what she'd done…

16

AVERY WAS FURIOUS. She hadn't expected her boss to air the feature so quickly. But another story had fallen through. A shorter one, so he'd cut too damn much out of her story in order to make it fit the time slot.

Poor Cody Mallehan had been cut. But his ego was healthy enough that he'd survive. Would she? She had a hollow achy feeling in her chest. Something she'd never felt before—until last night when Dawson hadn't showed up at her door. Maybe Fiona had warned him about the feature.

Avery should have. It would have been the right thing to do. She'd thought running the report was the right thing. Now she wasn't so certain.

Sure, her boss had been thrilled. He'd wanted her to cut her vacation short and return ASAP. She probably should have. But she wanted to see Dawson first. She wanted to make sure he didn't hate her.

But he wasn't at the firehouse. Or his cabin. "I can't find him anywhere," she told her sister as she walked into Kim's kitchen.

"You just missed him."

"Dawson?" Her heart shuddered now. "He was here? Was he looking for me?"

Kim shook her head. "He was picking up the boys for their camping trip."

"What?" She'd known nothing about it. But then, she'd been distracted.

"He probably didn't mention it for fear you'd run a story on it," Kim said. And there was thinly veiled disapproval in her voice.

"He rescued your sons," Avery said. "He deserved to get the credit for it."

"He deserved to have his privacy respected," Kim replied. "Like he wanted."

"You talked to him?" Avery asked. "How mad is he?"

Kim shrugged. "Not mad enough to cancel his trip with the boys."

Dawson wouldn't have done that. He was too good a man to take out what she'd done on her nephews. "Of course he wouldn't do that."

"Why did you?" Kim asked.

"I never agreed to go camping with them," Avery said. But maybe she should have…

"Why did you do the report?" Kim asked. "Even after you knew he didn't want the publicity."

Heat flushed Avery's face. "My career isn't going that great," she admitted. "They hired another reporter. I was already fighting for airtime. I was probably going to lose my job." She still could if she didn't return as her boss had asked.

"So you used him?"

"I—I—" She couldn't deny that she had. She'd tried to justify it. But it didn't change the fact that she'd known he hadn't wanted the publicity and she'd done the story anyway. She needed to apologize. "Do you have another sleeping bag?"

"What?" Kim asked.

"I need to use it," Avery said. She doubted Dawson would let her share his. But he couldn't kick her out of the woods. "And you need to tell me where they are."

Kim shook her head.

"I know you know," Avery said. "You probably had GPS chips implanted in the boys after the fire." She was surprised that Kim had even let them leave the house after Avery had brought up the possibility of an arsonist being in Northern Lakes. But Kim believed the campers had started the fire. Maybe that was why Dawson had taken them camping—to show them how to do it safely.

Kim sighed. "He's going to be furious…"

He was. When Avery drove the Jeep up to their campsite an hour later, she saw it on his face. His clenched jaw. The anger glinting in his topaz eyes.

"Aunt Avery?" Kade said, as if he couldn't believe it was her.

"What are you doing here?" Ian asked.

She'd never gone camping with them before, so of course they would question her appearance. They weren't any more welcoming than Dawson was. Probably because they didn't want to share his attention with her. Their father was gone so much they didn't have much of a male influence in their lives.

She felt another pang of guilt that she had intruded on their trip. "I brought chocolate and graham crackers for s'mores," she said. Usually she could get to them with sweets.

Predictably they both grinned. "You did?"

"They're in the back of the Jeep," she said. "Can you get everything and my sleeping bag?"

Dawson waited until the boys had hurried toward her Jeep before he said, "You're not staying."

"You don't own the forest," she said. Then she winced at her own petulant tone. She owed him an apology, not more attitude.

He nodded in agreement. "True. But I set up this campsite. And you're not welcome here."

The coldness of his voice made the hollow feeling in her chest intensify. She felt so empty. What had she done? "Dawson—"

Before she could begin the apology she owed him, the boys were back. "Look," Kade said as he dropped bags onto the ground. "Aunt Avery brought dark chocolate and milk chocolate and caramel…"

"I didn't know what you liked," she told Dawson. She knew her nephews loved it all. But she didn't know Dawson's preferences beyond the bedroom. She knew where he liked to be touched, where he liked to be kissed…

But she didn't know what he liked to eat. Or drink. Or what music he listened to. She really knew very little about him. An old transistor radio sat inside the tent, playing country music. It must have been his choice because the boys liked rap.

"You know what I don't like," he said. "I thought I made it very clear."

The boys glanced between them, their faces curious.

"You don't like s'mores?" Ian asked.

Dawson shook his head. "I don't like reporters."

"But Aunt Avery's a reporter," Kade said. "You don't like Aunt Avery?"

He chuckled bitterly, but he didn't answer her nephew.

"She made us all famous," Ian said. "She put us on TV."

"The fire happened a while ago," Dawson said. "There was no reason to bring it up again. No reason to bring up the past at all…"

He wasn't going to forgive her. It didn't matter how much she apologized. She had blown it with him. She drew in a shuddery breath. It had grown cold despite the fire he'd started.

"You know," she said, trying to hold her voice steady, "I better not stay. I have to get up early tomorrow and fly home." Because Chicago was home now. Northern Lakes was not and never would be again. Since her job was probably all she'd ever have, she needed to return to it.

She reached for her nephews. "So give me hugs in case I don't see you before I leave," she said.

This time they didn't fight her. They let her kiss their cheeks. They even hugged her tightly, as if they could somehow sense the pain she felt inside—the loss.

Whatever she could have had with Dawson she'd destroyed. She'd let her ambitions get in the way.

"What about Dawson?" Ian asked. "Aren't you going to give him a kiss goodbye?"

His body tensed. And she was sure he would refuse. But when he said nothing, she stepped forward, stood on tiptoe and pressed her lips to his cheek. Stubble had already broken through the skin, making his jaw dark and bristly. She found it as sexy as everything else about him. She whispered, "I'm sorry…"

But she wasn't sure if he heard her. Or if he cared. He said nothing to her as she walked away. He just let her go.

EVEN NOW, HOURS LATER, Dawson could feel the imprint of her lips against his cheek. As furious as he was with her, he'd been tempted to turn his head, tempted to let her lips brush over his.

She was leaving. He might never see her again. Sure, she would return to see her family. She obviously loved the twins and her sister. But he might not be here when she returned. He could be working a fire out West. Or in Canada, even…

He might only see her on the news from now on. The thought should have given him some relief, should have made him feel safer. He couldn't fall for her if he didn't see her. But it was too late.

He'd already fallen for her. Not that it mattered. She had to know doing the special feature on him would end whatever had started between them.

She didn't care about him. She'd only used him for her story. That was all she cared about, her career. He shuddered.

The boys were shivering, too, despite the heat blasting from the truck vents. Dawn had just barely broken when he pulled up in their driveway. The night had gotten unseasonably cold. They hadn't been equipped with the subzero temperature sleeping bags they'd had on the Boy Scout camping trip. So he'd decided to bring them home early.

It wasn't as if he'd gotten any sleep anyway. He'd lain awake, his body aching for Avery. Maybe he should have let her stay. But even if he'd agreed, she probably would have left Northern Lakes. He didn't doubt she was flying home to Chicago. There was no reason for her to stay here anymore.

She'd done her story. At least it had been on him and not the arsonist. If she'd given the arsonist the attention she'd given Dawson…

He shuddered again.

"You're cold, too?" Ian asked, his teeth chattering.

"Yes," Dawson said. "Sorry we weren't more prepared

for the trip, guys." He would have been had he not been so furious with their aunt. Then he might have checked the weather and known how low the temperature was going to drop. But he'd been preoccupied. "We'll do it again."

"We will?" Kade asked hopefully.

Dawson nodded. "Of course."

"But I thought you were mad at Aunt Avery," Ian said.

He was. He wouldn't lie to the boys and try to deny it. "I'm not mad at you two," he said.

"But we talked about you, too," Ian said.

Dawson felt a pang of regret. It was their story, too. They should have been able to tell it without feeling guilty about it. "That's fine," he assured them. "I'm okay with that." A tap on his window drew his attention from the boys. He rolled it down and Kim Pritchard leaned in.

"I have hot chocolate waiting for the two of you," she told the boys. As the back door of his quad cab pickup opened, she added, "Thank Mr. Hess for taking you camping."

"Thank you!" they called out in unison. But they headed quickly for the house.

"I have coffee, too, or more hot chocolate if you'd like," she offered him.

He shook his head.

Kim leaned farther into his open window and glanced around. "So did you kill her?" Obviously she'd seen the special feature and had known how opposed to it he'd been.

"No."

Finally Kim leaned back and studied his face. "She didn't crash your camping trip?"

He felt the muscle twitch along his jaw.

"Oh, she did," Kim said. "You sure you didn't kill

her? If I check their backpacks, will the boys have new badges for helping dispose of a body?"

A chuckle slipped out despite his effort to hold it in. He liked Avery's sister. Hell, most of the time he liked Avery…when she wasn't being a nosy reporter.

"She left on her own," he assured her sister. "Said she had an early flight."

Kim snorted. "First I've heard of it. And she would have had me drop her at the airport if she had a flight."

"I'm not surprised she'd lie," he said.

Kim smacked his shoulder. "My sister isn't a liar."

He arched a brow.

"Did she ever tell you she wouldn't do the feature?" Kim asked.

"No," he reluctantly admitted.

"Then she didn't lie to you," Kim pointed out. "And from what she told me, she needed a big story to keep her job at the station."

"What?"

"The news business is cutthroat," she explained. "She has to fight for airtime."

He'd had no idea. But it still didn't excuse what she'd done, how she'd used him. "I made it clear that I didn't want to be the focus of her feature," Dawson said. "And clearly she did lie about having a flight this morning."

Kim shrugged. "Maybe she didn't," she said. "She might have driven herself and left the Jeep at the airport."

The thought of her being gone had his shoulders slumping and Kim smiling. "What?" he asked at her odd reaction.

Her smile widened and she said, "You love her."

Feeling as if he'd been punched, Dawson gasped. Then he sucked in a breath to replace the one he'd expelled. And he smelled *it*. He dragged in a deep breath.

"I'm sorry," she said. "I didn't mean to make you hyperventilate."

Her comment had scared him. But what he smelled scared him more. He pushed open the driver's door and stepped out. It was early for someone to have started a bonfire—too late for one to still be burning from the night before. But it was cold so maybe someone had started a fire in their hearth. It didn't smell like just wood smoke to him, though. It smelled like gasoline.

He studied the sky on both sides of the road. It was just a puff—just a slight sheen of smoke rising above the trees. But he knew what it meant and he knew where it was coming from.

Kim reached out and grasped his arm as the realization dawned on her. Her voice rising with fear, she asked, "That's coming from Avery's place, isn't it?

The houses were far enough apart on the lake that there was no mistaking what was on fire.

Avery's cottage. And if she hadn't taken a flight out, Avery was probably asleep inside...

17

EVEN CLOSED, HER eyes began to burn; tears leaked out their corners. She blinked. But her vision didn't clear. Had she had a bad dream? Was she crying?

She'd felt like it last night when Dawson had been so cold to her, when he hadn't even given her a chance to apologize. But her nose burned, too. Then she drew in a breath that singed her lungs.

Smoke. Something was on fire. And it wasn't just a piece of paper burning in the fireplace. This was more than that.

The cottage was on fire.

She struggled to get up, but the sheets were tangled around her. She'd slept restlessly, involuntarily reaching out for Dawson. How had she gotten used to sleeping with him so quickly after all the years she'd slept alone?

She fell—hard—onto the floor. Her hand fumbled across something soft. A shirt had been left next to the bed. So had a pair of yoga pants. She dragged them on quickly. And then, staying close to the floor, she headed toward the window; it was her closest means of escape.

But when she pulled the curtains aside, she found the window was already black. The heat of the flames had scorched the glass. The fire was right outside her bed-room—the flames crackling as they began to consume the wood siding.

She screamed.

The person claiming to be the arsonist hadn't been is-suing empty threats. He'd been serious. She was afraid of him now—afraid of what he'd done. Too late, she realized she should have taken him seriously from the beginning. Gone to the police, or at least told Dawson.

Had he started a fire outside her every escape route? Was there no way out? The smoke filled her bedroom now. The only air she could breathe was at the floor. She got down on her belly and crawled toward the door.

Hopefully he hadn't gotten inside—hopefully he hadn't started a fire in the living room, too. Or maybe he was out there, waiting for her.

The crackling of the flames grew louder, but she heard a crash above that noise—one so loud the house shook. Had something exploded?

She had put herself in some dangerous situations be-fore to get a story. But she had never imagined that she might die like this. Her throat was burning, but she man-aged one more scream—just as the door to her bedroom flew open and slammed against the wall.

She could see boots—but just boots. The smoke ob-scured the rest of him except for a tall and bulky shadow. Was this the arsonist? Was he going to make certain his fire claimed a victim this time?

Strong hands grasped her arms. An arm wound be-neath her legs as she was lifted. She recognized those arms—that strength even before she got close enough to see his face. "Dawson…"

She'd thought he was out in the woods camping with the boys. How had he known she needed him?

He moved quickly, rushing back through her living room to the front door. It was morning. It had to be. But the smoke had darkened the sky.

"Did you call an ambulance?" he asked someone.

"Yes," Kim replied, her voice cracking with tears. "Is she…?"

She fought to lift her head—to meet her sister's gaze. "I'm…" She coughed, her throat and eyes continuing to burn.

Dawson laid her down on the ground. And she shivered with fear. Was he leaving her here? As angry as he'd been with her, she was surprised he'd rescued her at all.

But he was Dawson Hess. He couldn't stop himself from being a hero.

Her sister dropped to her knees beside her. "I called the ambulance. Help's coming."

She didn't need help. She just needed Dawson. Then he was back—with an oxygen mask he put over her mouth and nose. The burst of clean air made her cough some more before she could actually manage to take it into her burning lungs.

She pulled the mask aside to murmur, "My house…" She loved that little colorful cottage. Had the flames consumed it already—the way they would have consumed her if Dawson hadn't broken in her front door? It dangled from damaged hinges. So much for her new dead bolt…

He slipped away again. But he didn't come back to her—he moved toward the house. Where was he going? He had something in his hand, but she couldn't figure out what. Tears still streaming from her eyes, she couldn't see clearly. But she couldn't miss when he walked back into the cottage—back into the fire.

She pulled the mask aside again to scream. "No!" But her voice was just a raspy whisper.

Kim's arm slid around her shoulders. "You'll be okay."

She wasn't worried about herself. She was worried about him.

"I hear the sirens now," Kim said.

Avery could hear nothing but the crackling of the flames and her pulse pounding in her ears. "Dawson…"

Kim glanced nervously toward the house, too. "I think he's trying to put out the fire."

But it was too big. And he didn't have his equipment. He had already risked his life to save hers. He didn't need to save her house. It was just a house. He was so much more important. Finally Avery heard the sirens, too. She hoped it was the rest of the crew—that they would save him as he'd saved her.

DAWSON THOUGHT HE'D been angry with her for running that special feature on him. That was nothing compared to how furious he was now. Thankfully the doctor had just given her a clean bill of health—because he intended to kill her.

But he hesitated outside her hospital room, trying to slow his racing heart. And voices drifted out to him.

"You're lucky Dawson brought the boys back early," Kim said, and her voice cracked with emotion. "He's the one who noticed the smoke."

Her voice raspy from that smoke, Avery replied, "I'm almost surprised he rescued me. He was furious with me for doing that story on him."

Dawson pushed open the door and stepped into the room. Both women turned to him with wide eyes. "That was nothing compared to how mad I am now," he said. And he slapped a piece of paper onto the tray across her bed.

When he focused on her—looking so slight and vulnerable propped against the pillows in the hospital bed—

his anger evaporated, leaving him with only what he'd felt that morning. Fear.

"What's that?" Kim asked.

But Avery didn't. She knew. "Where'd you find it?" she asked instead.

"This one was under your door," he said. "I didn't notice it when I broke it down. I didn't notice it until I went back inside to try to put out the fire."

"You shouldn't have gone back inside," she said. "It's just a house."

"It's just my job," he reminded her. He stopped fires— no matter where they were or how dangerous. He'd had some equipment in the back of the truck. Oxygen and an extinguisher.

"You could have been killed," she said.

He tapped the paper. "And so could you."

"What is that?" Kim asked again.

Dawson flipped open the paper and read aloud, "'Miss Kincaid, you are wasting your time with stories about your boyfriend. You're a joke as a journalist. I am the real story. If you won't report about me, you won't report about anyone anymore.'"

Kim gasped. "Avery! You're in danger!"

Avery shook her head. "No…"

His hand shook as he folded the paper over again. "He tried to kill you!"

She shivered. And he regretted his harshness. She had already been through so much. But if she'd been open about her contact with the arsonist, he could have protected her. He could have made certain she was never in danger—the way she'd been that morning.

He brought her purse from where he'd been holding it behind his back. He had retrieved that, too. "There are two more notes inside."

She gasped. "You went through my purse?"

He'd been inside her body. Had pulled her out of a burning house. What the hell did she care about her purse? He would never understand women.

"You went through my drawers," he said.

Kim gasped. "Maybe I should leave—"

"The drawers beneath my bed," he explained. "I had a scrapbook in one of them." That must have been how she'd found out about Martin. "You snooped through my whole house."

Her face flushed.

"And you should have turned over these letters long ago," he said.

"I only got the first one a couple of days ago," she said.

Kim nodded. "When you asked me about the fire. That's your source? An anonymous note?"

More like ominous. He'd threatened her. And he'd made good on that threat.

A fist knocked on the door to her room.

"Come in," she called out, almost eagerly. She obviously didn't want to talk about the notes she'd been receiving or she would have brought them up days ago.

She should have.

The door opened to Zimmer's serious face. Cody and Wyatt filed in behind their boss. "Are you okay, Ms. Kincaid?" Braden asked.

She nodded. "What about my house?"

"The fire's out," Wyatt said. "It was pretty much out when we got there thanks to Dawson spraying the fire retardant around." He turned toward him and added, "There really isn't much damage—just that side wall of the bedroom."

Where she'd been sleeping...

If he hadn't made her leave the campsite, she would

have been with him. He shouldn't have made her leave. He hadn't known about the notes. But he'd been pretty certain that someone had been inside her house, had been watching her from behind the trees in her yard. He should have made certain she was safe until she got on that plane to Chicago.

"There was so much smoke," Avery murmured. Her eyes narrowed with suspicion. "How could there not be much damage?"

She thought his friends were lying to her.

"There was more smoke than flames," he explained. He'd seen that when he'd put it out. The smoke had come from the gasoline-soaked hay bales that had been lit right outside her bedroom window.

"We should discuss the details outside," Braden said. "So we don't disturb Ms. Kincaid. She's already been through a lot."

Dawson sighed. "She knows." He handed the letters over to his boss. "The arsonist has been sending her notes."

Zimmer glanced over the pages. "Threatening notes…"

"He tried to kill her," Dawson said. And he knew why—because she'd run the special feature on Dawson rather than reporting about the Northern Lakes arsonist.

"No," she said, probably to soothe her sister's fears. After what had happened, she couldn't deny that she was. And she couldn't deny what she knew.

Neither could they.

"She is in danger," he said. "That's why she needs to leave now. The doctor said her lungs are fine. He will sign her release."

"But my house…" Avery murmured.

"Can be fixed when you're back in Chicago," Dawson said. He had to believe she would be safer there than in Northern Lakes. The arsonist wasn't likely to follow her to Chicago. If the hot spots were anything to go by, so far he had stuck around the village. "You need to go *home*, Avery."

Her eyes widened with confusion. "Home?"

"To Chicago," he said. "This isn't your home. This is just the place you came to track down a story." And she'd done her job as well as she always seemed to do. She'd tracked down the story so well that she'd nearly gotten killed.

He didn't care now that she'd done the report about him. He didn't even care if she reported about the arsonist. But he refrained from telling her that—especially in front of his coworkers. He could feel Zimmer's anxiety. Even though the superintendent had suspected that the arsonist had contacted her, he'd hoped it wasn't true. He kept reading and rereading the notes he held.

But Dawson ignored him and the other two men. He turned to her sister instead. "You tell her," he urged Kim. "She's in danger here. And her being here will put you and your kids in danger, too."

Kim's eyes widened with fear now. She'd already almost lost her sons.

Avery gasped. "I would never—"

"You will if you stay here," he said.

He needed to get her to leave—for her safety more than her sister's or the boys'. In order to protect her, he had to let her go. Not that he'd ever truly had her. She'd never really been his. She'd only been using him. But he didn't care about that now. He cared only about making sure she didn't get hurt physically. But in order to do that, he might need to hurt her emotionally.

So he drew in a deep breath and forced himself to be cruel. "You need to get the hell out of Northern Lakes. Now."

18

AVERY HAD SEEN Dawson furious. She'd seen him passionate. She'd seen him brave and stoic. She'd never seen him like this—so cold. Colder even than he'd been the night before at the campsite. So cold she shivered.

Kim pulled up a blanket for her, but as she did, her hands shook. He had scared her sister. And Kim had already endured enough fear to last her a lifetime.

"You shouldn't have said that," she chastised him.

"What?" he asked. "The truth? The whole damn town knows you don't belong here anymore. Just go back to your big city and your big career, Avery, and leave the rest of us alone."

Tears stung her eyes, so she squeezed them shut. She knew now that he would never forgive her for doing that special feature. Whatever they might have had was ruined; she'd ruined it. When she opened her eyes again, he was gone.

Cody and Wyatt had left, too. But Superintendent Zimmer had stayed behind—along with her nervous sister.

"He's wrong," she told Kim. "I'm not putting you and the boys in any danger."

But Kim wouldn't meet her gaze. She glanced at the superintendent instead—as if seeking his assurance. "Was it arson?" she asked.

"Today?" He nodded. "Definitely."

"The other fire," she said. "The one that would have killed my kids if Dawson and the others hadn't saved them. Was that fire arson?"

Superintendent Zimmer glanced to Avery and shook his head.

"So, no?" she asked, almost hopefully.

Of course it was better to think that the fire had been an accident than that someone had deliberately tried to kill her children.

"Was Dawson wrong?" Kim asked.

Zimmer hesitated. He probably didn't want to contradict his assistant superintendent, but he wasn't willing to admit the truth, either.

"He won't answer you in front of me," Avery said. "If he confirms that it was, I can run the story." That was why the report hadn't been made official. After the state police had told her the US Forest Service was in charge of the investigation, she'd checked with them and been told it was ongoing.

Despite the Freedom of Information Act, the government agency could exempt reports from disclosure if the public learning anything would compromise an ongoing investigation.

"Even if you had confirmation," Zimmer carefully replied, "you would be foolish to run a story about an arsonist."

"Why?" she asked. "Because then the public could be more vigilant? Because then they could protect themselves from a future fire?"

"You knew," he said. "You couldn't protect yourself."

"I didn't do what he wanted," she said. "I didn't run the story about him." She'd run it about Dawson, instead. And she'd pissed off both of them.

Zimmer nodded. "That's what feeds an arsonist," he said. "If you give him any attention, he'll start more fires. He'll want more and more attention. It'll never be enough."

Kind of like her and Dawson. No matter how many times they'd made love, it had never been enough. At least, it hadn't been for her. Apparently he'd had enough because he wanted her gone.

"Dawson was right," his boss said. "You should go back to Chicago. Your being here incited him—gave him reason to hope that he'd get that attention."

"So you're saying everyone will be safer if I leave?" she asked.

Zimmer gave her a grim nod.

"I wasn't here when he started that first fire," she pointed out. And now she was angry. "I wasn't here when the previous hot spots flared up, either. I'm not letting you or Dawson blame me for what this guy has done."

Kim reached out and squeezed her hand. "Nobody's blaming you."

Despite her sister's reassurance, Avery wondered if Kim didn't want her to leave, too—like everyone else. Her heart ached over Dawson's coldness and what he'd told her. Until he'd said that Northern Lakes wasn't her home, she hadn't realized how much she'd wanted it to be. There were no opportunities for her here, though. Career or otherwise.

And if she didn't go back soon, she would probably lose her job.

"What about the story, Ms. Kincaid?" Zimmer asked.

Her head began to pound with weariness and from the smoke. "Will you confirm that it was arson?" she asked.

"I told you why I won't," he replied. "I believe it will put the town in more danger."

"Then I can't run the story," she said.

Kim squeezed her hand. "But won't that put you in more danger? Won't he try to kill you again?"

She was afraid, but she refused to show that to her sister. So she just shrugged. "I can't run an unsubstantiated story."

Zimmer expelled a shaky breath. "Thank you. And I'll make sure that if you decide to stay, you'll have protection."

Like her, he knew it wouldn't be Dawson. She doubted he would be her hero ever again.

"WHAT THE HELL are you doing here?" Dawson asked the minute she opened the new door to her cottage. He'd broken down her last one. He'd been tempted to break down this one, too—swing her over his shoulder and haul her off to the airport.

But now that she'd opened it, he just wanted to haul her off to the bedroom. She looked beautiful and more vulnerable than he'd ever seen her. Her skin was pale; she hadn't completely recovered from the smoke inhalation she'd suffered.

"This is my home," she replied defiantly. "No matter what you say."

He'd struck a nerve when he'd said that—one he hadn't expected. He'd just wanted to convince her to leave, to go back to Chicago. Maybe he hadn't been trying to protect only her when he'd done that. Maybe he'd been trying to protect himself, too.

"Your life isn't here," he said. And he worried that if

she stayed, she wouldn't have a life. The arsonist would end it for her unless…

"I have more here than you do," she said. "I grew up here. I have my family here."

"My friends and my job are here," he said. "So you're just giving up your career, then?"

"Of course not."

"But you haven't gone back to Chicago."

"I wasn't in Chicago when I did the special feature on you," she pointed out.

"So you're still working," he said. "You're doing a report about the arson?"

She shook her head.

"Why the hell not?" he asked. And his fury returned. Was she deliberately taunting the arsonist? The note had been clear; he wanted her to report that the fire was arson or he would hurt her.

Her brow furrowed with confusion. "Because your boss explained why I shouldn't."

"I told you not to run the report on me and you ran it anyway," he said. And his pain and resentment returned. He could never trust her again. But even still, he couldn't stop himself from caring about her—about her safety.

"This is a little different," she murmured.

"Damn Zimmer," he said. It wasn't fair for the superintendent to risk her life. "He's putting you in danger."

"Better me than more innocent lives," she said. "And why do you care whether or not I'm in danger?"

"Because I…" Why did he? Did he love her? He refused to consider it. He couldn't give his heart to a woman he didn't trust. When she'd run that report, she'd betrayed him. Maybe she hadn't made any promises to him. Maybe she hadn't lied to him. But she'd known he didn't want the media attention and she'd run the story anyway.

"What?" she persisted. And she leaned toward him, as if eager for his answer. "I thought you were furious with me."

"I am," he said. "And you knew I would be."

"I thought you would change your mind about the special feature," she said, "once you saw it."

The report had been a great tribute to Martin in a way. But it had also brought up that pain again. "You thought it would get you more airtime," he said. "That was the only reason you did it. For your career."

"Dawson—"

"Ironically you could have cost me mine."

She tensed. "What do you mean?"

"No one knew about the connection between me and Wyatt," he said. "I was lucky Zimmer didn't kick me off the team. I'm lucky Wyatt didn't ask him to."

She gasped. "I—I am so sorry. I didn't realize—"

"Maybe you should have done a little more research," he suggested.

"I would have," she said. "If you would have talked to me." She stepped closer to him. "This is the most you've talked to me."

"I just…" He wasn't much of a talker because it wasn't easy for him to express himself with words. It was easier for him to show her how he felt. So he reached out and brushed his fingertips across her cheek.

She gasped at the touch, and her face grew paler than it had been.

"Are you okay?" he asked. Maybe she was still suffering from the smoke inhalation.

She shook her head. "No," she said. "Because I don't

think it'll matter how many times I apologize. I don't think you'll ever forgive me."

He could forgive her; he just wouldn't be able to trust her again. "Avery…"

"Please," she murmured. She stepped closer, stood on tiptoe and brushed her lips along his jaw. "Please forgive me…"

He lowered his head so that her lips brushed across his. There was a tenderness to their kiss that had never been there before. He had come too close to losing her—not just to Chicago and her career, but forever.

If her sister hadn't kept him talking…

If he hadn't smelled the smoke…

If Avery hadn't awakened and gotten down on the floor…

"I can forgive you," he said, "if you leave."

She pulled back. And her turquoise eyes were bright with tears.

"You really want me gone that badly?"

"I really want you safe that badly," he admitted.

Her lips curved into a smile. "You care about me," she said.

"Of course I care."

"I care, too," she said. "I've missed you…"

He had missed her, too. So badly…

He kissed her again—passionately. His body tensed, the ache he'd felt the past couple of days intensifying.

She caught his hand in hers and tugged him toward the other side of the house. "I've been using the bedroom on this side."

She led him to the second bedroom. It was smaller than the smoke-damaged one. An old brass bed nearly filled it. She tugged him toward the bed, but it was as if the effort exhausted her because she settled onto the edge of the mattress. And the ancient frame creaked.

He dropped to his knees in front of her. "Are you really all right?"

"I'm fine," she told him. "Completely recovered."

"It's only been a couple of days…" A couple of days that he'd worried about her constantly. A couple of days until he'd dropped by her sister's with the excuse of visiting the boys. Kim hadn't been fooled, and she'd quickly shared with him that Avery hadn't left. And that she'd insisted on staying in her smoke-damaged house rather than moving in with her. She hadn't wanted to risk the safety of Kim or the boys. And she had asked Zimmer to send the state police officer he had offered for her protection to her sister's.

"I'm fine," she insisted. "Or I will be if you forgive me…"

"You will be if you leave," he said. "You need to go back to Chicago."

She shook her head.

"Kim told me your boss ordered you back." Her job meant everything to her, so why was she risking it?

Unless she was compiling more details to report about the arsonist?

"I'll leave soon," she said. "But I don't want to leave with you angry with me."

All that anger and betrayal he'd felt began to ebb away. He touched her face again, skimming his fingertips along her jaw.

"Avery…"

"Never thought I'd say this to you," she remarked. "But you talk too much." She locked her arms around his neck and pulled his head close for her kiss.

Her tongue teased him, skimming across his lower lip. He groaned.

It was goodbye. That was what he told himself. She would leave for Chicago, and he would never see her again. Touch her again…

He would let her go. And she would be safe. But first he had to be with her one last time. He pulled her shirt up and over her head. Her blond hair fell like silk back around her shoulders. She wore a bra, but it was another one of those nearly transparent lacy ones. He quickly unclasped it so it dropped away. And he cupped her breasts in his hands, gently caressing them. His thumb flicked over her nipples.

She moaned. Then she tugged up his T-shirt and pulled it off his head. Rubbing her breasts against the hair on his chest, she moaned again. Then she reached for his zipper.

He caught her hand in his. He wanted this moment to last. So he pushed her gently back onto the bed. Then he pulled off her shorts. Her legs were so long, so sexy. He dropped kisses along each one. Then he trailed his tongue up her inner thigh.

She trembled and shifted against the bed, making it creak. "Dawson…" she murmured.

"You talk too much," he admonished her. He wanted her beyond speech—wanted her capable only of moaning and screaming. He took his time, running his hands over every inch of her silky skin. He slid his tongue across her but he didn't touch her clit.

She arched up and whimpered. "Please…"

But he'd gone back to her breasts. He used his tongue on her nipples, lapping at them until she shuddered and uttered a tiny cry.

It wasn't enough. He wanted more—wanted to give her more. So he moved his mouth lower, back between her thighs. And he stroked his tongue over her. Then he thrust it inside her.

"Dawson…" Her fingers clutched at his hair, but she wasn't trying to pull him away. She was urging him closer. He moved his hand over her, rubbing her clit with his thumb while he continued to stroke his tongue inside her.

She cried out again as she came, shuddering beneath his touch and his mouth. His control snapped. He had to be inside her. So he kicked off his jeans and boxers and rolled the condom over his pulsing cock.

He lifted her legs, sliding them over his shoulders, before burying himself inside her. Those inner muscles of hers contracted, clutching him. Then her hands slid down his chest, her nails scraping across his nipples.

He moved inside her, sliding deeper. She thrust up, matching his frantic rhythm. They hung tightly to each other as they raced toward release. The tension inside Dawson was unbearable—more intense than anything he'd felt before.

Her nails dug in and she screamed. That was the scream he loved hearing from her—the one of intense pleasure. Not the one he'd heard the day of the fire—the scream of fear while she gasped for breath on her smoke-filled bedroom's floor.

If he'd lost her…

"Dawson…" she murmured his name, probably surprised that he had stopped moving.

He was still hard, still pulsing inside her. He needed to come, too. He needed her. He began to move again, sliding in and out. But he did it slowly—with long strokes.

Pretty soon she was breathing hard again, clutching at him again. Her eyes widened with shock as she came once more. This time he joined her, letting his control slip for just a moment as pleasure overwhelmed him.

But it was more than pleasure. It was love, just as Kim had guessed. Even though he knew he couldn't trust Avery—couldn't be with her—he'd fallen for her.

_19_

AVERY SNUGGLED AGAINST Dawson's chest, his arm wound tightly—protectively—around her. She knew now why he'd said everything he had in the hospital. He'd wanted her to leave because he'd been worried about her.

He'd even admitted that he cared. She cared, too.

He pulled her more closely against him. "I can't believe Zimmer told you not to run the story."

"You know why," she said. "It's why you tried keeping it from me that the fire was arson. You didn't want to feed the arsonist's need for attention."

"I still don't," he admitted. "But I don't want you in danger, either."

She pressed a kiss to his chest and said, "I feel very safe with you." And she did.

She wasn't sure now if Northern Lakes was home to her. Or his arms.

He cursed. "I should have been with you the minute you got out of the hospital."

"Superintendent Zimmer has a state police officer watching over me and making sure the arsonist doesn't try to hurt me again." She'd tried to refuse the protection though. But Zimmer had been persistent, so she'd made him post one near her sister's, too.

Dawson snorted. "A police officer doesn't know how to handle an arsonist. What if he started another fire? What would a cop do?"

"Call you," she said with a smile. Just as she'd never heard him sound as cold as he had in the hospital, she'd never heard him sound like this—almost jealous.

"So let's cut out the middle man," he suggested. "Until you can get a flight back to Chicago, I will stay with you."

The hurt flashed through her again. Maybe he didn't care. "You still want me to return to Chicago?"

His arm contracted—almost of its own volition— pulling her closer. "Yes, you have to. As soon as possible."

Her boss had wanted her back even before her week was up. But she had stalled, saying that she had to set up a contractor to repair her cottage. She'd actually been hoping Dawson would come around again, that he would forgive her. But even though they'd made love, she still wasn't certain he'd forgiven her. "I have to get a contractor started on the smoke damage before I leave."

"You really do love this place," he said.

She was beginning to worry that it wasn't all she loved.

"Thank you," she said.

"For what?"

"For putting out the fire," she said. "If you hadn't, the cottage might have been a total loss."

"I want to put out the fire," he said. "But every time I touch you, it starts up again—hotter than before."

Her breath escaped in a shaky sigh. "It does," she agreed. She had never felt anything as powerful as the attraction between them.

"Like right now," he said. "I just want to lie here with you in my arms, your head on my chest..." He clasped her hand, sliding it down his chest to his hard cock. "But I can't touch you and not want you."

"I want you, too," she said. Her clit began to throb as desire overwhelmed her. She slid her hand around his erection and stroked up and down the length of him.

She didn't want to leave him.

He groaned. "Staying with you to make sure you're safe until you leave…" He groaned again as she continued to pump him. "It's going to be a sacrifice but…"

"It's a sacrifice you're willing to make?" she teased.

He leaned down and kissed her. "Very willing," he murmured.

He was still her hero.

She squirmed in his arms, moving down his body, so that she could use her mouth on him, too. She sucked on the tip as she continued to stroke the length of him.

He groaned again as sweat began to bead on his brow and upper lip. "Avery…"

His body was tense. He was close to coming—close to taking the pleasure she wanted to give him. Then that damn siren went off.

He jerked upright and cursed.

"Dawson," she said. "Let me finish…" She couldn't imagine letting him go, as close as he was—as badly as he needed release.

He groaned. But his hands gripped her shoulders and moved her away from him. "I have to leave."

"But…"

He dressed quickly—so quickly that his shirt was inside out, and his jeans weren't zipped all the way. But maybe that was because he was still hard.

"Y—you…" she stammered.

He leaned down and kissed her lips. "I have to go," he said. "That siren means it's a big one."

Before she could protest further, he was gone. She heard his truck's engine roar as he sped down the driveway, heard the tires squeal as he turned onto the road. She could even feel the urgency he'd felt. The siren had sounded different than when she'd heard it before. It had been louder, longer, more intense. A big fire.

Fear coursed through her as she remembered awakening to smoke and the window being blocked. That had been a little fire. What would a big fire be like?

She'd reported on the big fire that had destroyed so much of the forest and nearly killed her nephews, as well. But she hadn't been allowed close to it. She'd seen more when her plane had flown over the fire as they were landing. And she'd seen the smoke. It had been everywhere—as if the town was fogged in for days.

It was late. But she wasn't going to sleep—and not just because she had a potential story to report. She wasn't going to sleep because Dawson was out there, in the middle of a big blaze.

She dressed quickly and grabbed the keys for her rental car. By the time she made it to the firehouse, all the engines were gone. Only the curly-haired kid stood in the empty garage.

"I'm not supposed to tell you where they went."

She smiled. As anxious as they'd been to get to the fire, they had taken the time to tell the kid not to talk to her. Dawson knew her well; he knew she would follow him. He just didn't know why.

It wasn't just because of the story now. It was because of *him*. She wanted to make sure he was okay.

Smoke was everywhere again, the sky so dark she couldn't tell where the fire was.

"Maybe I came to see you," she told him.

His face flushed.

She'd asked him his name before. But she struggled to remember it for a moment. "Stanley…" It was such an old-fashioned name for a teenager.

"Assistant Superintendent Hess warned me that you'd be extra nice to get me to tell you where they are."

Dawson definitely knew her well.

"He did?"

"But it's too dangerous for you to go there, so I can't tell you," Stanley said.

Her heart had been pounding fast since the siren had gone off; it began to pound even faster now. Dawson was in danger.

A clicking noise drew her attention to the open doors of the garage. A woman walked up the short drive, her heels snapping against the concrete. "Hey," Fiona O'Brien said. "I thought you would have left town after the fire."

"I'm not letting an arsonist chase me away from my home," Avery said.

"Just burn you out of it?" Fiona asked.

"He tried," Avery admitted. "But it's only minor damage."

"It could have been worse…"

"Like this fire?" she asked.

Fiona's green eyes were dark and her face pale.

"Dawson said it was a big one," Avery said, "when he left."

"He was with you when the siren sounded?"

Avery nodded.

"I didn't think he would forgive you for that special feature."

"I don't think he has," Avery said, expressing her other fear aloud. He'd made love to her, but she'd pretty much thrown herself at him. His only real concern had been her safety. But she couldn't take that personally; Dawson rescued everyone. "But that's the least of my concerns right now."

Fiona looked up at the dark sky, too, and her face grew tense with worry.

"You must really love Wyatt a lot," Avery said. "I can tell this is killing you—worrying about him. You didn't want your brother to become a firefighter because of the danger, but then you fell for a Hotshot."

Fiona released a shaky little breath. "Wyatt is worth all the worry," she said. "Not that I have any reason to worry. Wyatt and the rest of the crew—they're highly trained and they work well together."

The same had been true of other Hotshot teams, but they'd lost members. Several years ago an entire team had been killed when the fire had jumped and turned on them. And more recently another team had lost a member in the wildfires out West.

"They protect each other," Fiona continued.

And everyone else.

"Wyatt will come home to me," Fiona said. And as she said it, she lifted her head. It was as if the worry fell off her. Only confidence remained, confidence in her fiancé and their love.

Avery envied her that confidence. She had no confidence in Dawson's feelings. Sure, he cared about her. But he cared about and took care of everyone. It was who he was as much as it was his job.

While she now realized Northern Lakes was home, it wasn't where she lived. She had to go back to Chicago and there was no way Dawson would join her there. Dawson's team was his family; he wouldn't give them up. And she wouldn't give up her career.

He would come home from the big fire, but he wouldn't be coming home to her.

THE FIRE WAS even worse than Dawson had imagined. The sky wasn't black with smoke; it glowed red as the flames rose all around them. There were several points of origin. So it couldn't have been a lightning strike—even if there'd actually been a storm, which there hadn't. The fire roared as it consumed the trees in the national forest. They'd saved these trees last time. This area of the forest hadn't been touched.

Until tonight.

Tonight it was being devoured. They'd brought in a helicopter to drop water on it. They had the dozers and the backhoes to make the breaks. But the fire was everywhere. Everywhere they turned…

Dawson couldn't even hear the engine of the dozer he was running. He couldn't hear anything but the fire—the ferocious roar of it.

Fear gripped him. But it wasn't fear for himself. It was fear for Avery. Hopefully she hadn't sweet-talked that damn kid into telling her where the fire was. But hell, Stanley wouldn't have had to say anything. No matter where she was in Northern Lakes, she would be able to see the smoke and probably even the flames.

She shouldn't be in Northern Lakes. She should be back in Chicago. But would she be safe there? The arsonist could follow her. It was obvious he would do anything to get the attention he craved. But his focus seemed to be Northern Lakes.

Dawson believed he'd set this fire. There were too many points of origin for a natural fire—it was coming from too many directions, turning on them.

Like the flames, his fear grew. And now it was for his team. Would they all get out of this alive?

20

AVERY STARED AT the TV mounted over her fireplace. For once she was watching the news instead of reporting it. She could have called her boss at the station, could have had the young male reporter sidelined while she reported about the latest wildfire consuming Huron National Forest. But she'd known she wouldn't be able to do what he was; she wouldn't be able to unemotionally report the news.

Fiona thought Avery had betrayed her feelings in the special feature on Dawson. Avery definitely would have done so if she'd reported what Clay was reporting live now.

"While battling this latest blaze to hit the forest in the past few months, a firefighter from the local Huron Hotshots has been critically injured."

Tears began to stream down her face. It had to be Dawson. He always went back for others, made sure everyone in danger got back to safety. Everyone but himself…

"We've spoken to a source at the local firehouse and learned that the prognosis isn't good for this firefighter," Clay continued. "He may have already succumbed to his injuries."

Her heart lurched as pain squeezed it. Damn it. Damn it.

She loved Dawson. For the first time in her life she'd fallen in love. And before she'd even realized it, she'd lost him.

She needed to go back to the firehouse. Ironically she'd left it when the news crews had rolled in. She hadn't wanted to be on the news when she wasn't reporting it. She hadn't wanted her concern for Dawson laid bare for everyone to see.

She understood his anger now over what she'd done—how she'd exposed his life. She'd thought she was doing the right thing, giving him the accolades he deserved. She'd only angered and embarrassed him. She'd even endangered his job.

But she didn't care who saw her now. She had to go back to the firehouse. She needed to talk to Clay's source herself. It couldn't be true…

Dawson was a hero—just like his stepfather had been. Had Dawson died as Martin Spedoske had? Saving others?

She couldn't stop crying; the tears just kept flowing down her face. Her nose burned, too. And her throat.

It was the smoke. It hung over the entire village like an eerie cloud of doom.

She needed to know for certain who the injured firefighter was and if he was still alive. She clicked off the television and turned for the door. That was when she saw it—the smoke pouring beneath it. It was too much to be from the fire miles away.

This fire was close—as close as the one had been outside her bedroom window.

A little scream slipped from her throat. She whirled toward the sliders. But when she dragged back the curtains—she saw only flames—rising from the bales of hay someone had put on the deck.

How had she not heard anything?

She'd been so engrossed in the news. So focused on the television—on finding out if Dawson was safe. She hadn't realized that she was in danger now. Of course the state police officers had left a while ago in order to help contain the fire.

The fire had found her—enveloping her as it had them. That was what Clay had reported, that the fire had surrounded the Hotshot crew—giving them no escape.

Dawson had been instrumental in getting her nephews out alive. Couldn't he have gotten out alive this time, too?

She needed him now—needed him to save her as he had last time. But if he was gone…

She had only herself to count on—which was the way she'd lived most of her adult life. She was smart. Independent. Resourceful.

And so scared she could barely think. She stepped back from the sliders, already able to feel the heat through the glass. There had to be another way out.

The one end of the house had already been damaged; the window was still boarded up. So she turned toward the other. But before she opened the bedroom door, she felt it—felt the heat against it.

The fire had already made it through the outside wall—was already inside the room where she'd been sleeping—where she'd made love with Dawson in the creaky antique bed.

Coughing and sputtering, she backed away from it. She needed to get down on the ground again—needed to try to find fresh air. But with the smoke billowing under the front door, there was no breathable air down there.

She screamed again. Not that anyone would hear her.

The neighbors were too far away. And the fire was getting loud. Glass tinkled as it began to break. Then there was a louder crack and a blade cut through the side of the house.

Wood splintered then broke down as the ax continued to chop its way through the wall. Finally there was a hole big enough for a man to step inside—his face was black from smoke. But his eyes were light—glittering amber.

She ran for the opening and flung her arms around his neck. "You're alive."

He wrapped his arms around her and pulled her out. He didn't speak. He just carried her halfway down the driveway to where the US Forest Service truck was parked.

Was he alive? Or was she only imagining that he'd come to her rescue? She reached out and touched his soot-covered jaw. It was so hard beneath her fingertips and rough with stubble.

"Are you alive?" she asked.

He glanced down at her in surprise—as if he thought she'd lost her mind. "Yes, I'm alive."

"Then who was hurt?"

His brow furrowed as he stared down at her.

"The news reported that a Hotshot had been critically injured," she said. "Who was it? Cody? Wyatt?" Not Wyatt. Fiona would be devastated. She couldn't have lost her fiancé.

He shook his head and assured her, "The rest of the team is fine."

"It *was* you!" she exclaimed. She blinked the smoke tears from her eyes and focused on him.

"I'm fine," he assured her. "Nobody was injured."

"But the news…"

"Got it wrong," he told her.

"But there was a source…" Her gaze met his as they both realized who that source was: the arsonist.

Had he wanted everyone to believe he'd killed a Hotshot or just her? Had he wanted her devastated before he killed her, too?

DAWSON CARRIED AVERY'S wriggling body through the door of his cabin. "I can walk," she protested. "The doctor said I'm fine."

He'd taken her to the ER to have her checked for smoke inhalation. She hadn't suffered any physical side effects. But Dawson worried about the emotional damage.

Maybe that was more his than hers, though. He'd heard her screaming inside that burning cottage. He'd heard the terror in her voice; it had echoed the terror in his heart. He'd never swung an ax as fast or hard as he had at the side of her house.

If the ax hadn't been in the truck, he might have torn the structure apart with his bare hands to get to her. That was why he carried her—because he didn't want to let her go. Even though he knew that he would have to…

He forced his arms to release her as he set her on her feet and stepped back. "I shouldn't have brought you here," he said.

She glanced outside his window. "The fire wasn't in this area, though."

No. It had been at the other end of the forest, where it had destroyed Cody's cabin.

"We should be safe here," she said.

Dawson shook his head. "I doubt you're going to be safe anyplace until we catch the arsonist."

She shivered. But she knew it. That was why she'd refused to go home with her distraught sister. Kim had wanted her to stay with them. She'd been upset that Avery had been left alone again.

But every firefighter and police officer had been needed to contain the forest fire. Was that why the arsonist had started it? Not just for the attention but also for the distraction?

While everyone had been focused on the fire, he'd gone after Avery again. And he'd almost succeeded this time.

"Was there a note?" she asked.

He shrugged. "Not that I saw." But the place had gone up fast. Unlike the previous fire, this one had done substantial damage. Her little cottage was a total loss. "But I think he knew you'd get his message even if he didn't leave it in writing."

She shivered again. "He wants me dead."

Dawson couldn't leave her standing there—cold and scared. He wrapped his arms around her.

Her breath shuddered out against his throat. "This is what I need," she murmured. "You to hold me."

There was nothing he wanted more. Well, there was one thing: her safety.

"You need to do it," he said.

She reached for his zipper, tugging it down. But he caught her hand. "Not that..." But he wanted her. He needed her—because he wasn't sure if he'd ever be with her again.

"You need to do a story about him, or at least say the fires are the work of an arsonist," Dawson said. "It's the only way to stop him."

She gasped. "Superintendent Zimmer thinks it'll make him more dangerous."

"He couldn't be much more dangerous," he said. Unless he killed her. And that couldn't happen.

"I can't take that risk," she said.

"I will," he said. "If you won't do it, I'll give the story to another reporter."

She snorted. "Which one? Clay may not have a job after reporting a lie."

Zimmer had interrogated the young reporter, who'd admitted no one at the firehouse had told him the Hotshots were trapped in the blaze. He'd received a call instead, which they later learned had come from a payphone near the firehouse. Anyone could have made that call. Clay hadn't even been able to say if the voice had been male or female.

Dawson threatened her with, "I'll give the story to that hot brunette who works for the station out of Detroit."

She tensed. "Caitlin Clark—my replacement?"

"Does she have long legs and a tight—"

She smacked his shoulder. "Dawson!"

"You don't think you're the only hot reporter, do you?" he teased.

"I thought you hated reporters."

"Most of them," he said. "But there's one…" One he'd actually fallen in love with. He loved Avery Kincaid. That was why he would do anything to keep her alive.

"Caitlin Clark?" Her chin lifted with pride and something flashed through her turquoise eyes, making them look greener: jealousy.

He nearly laughed. But he needed to make his point first.

"I have better legs," she said haughtily.

He knew it. "Prove it," he said.

She reached for the button of her jeans. But he caught her hand. If she undressed now, he'd lose his focus. He had to get her to agree to report the story.

"Get cleaned up and get into one of your skintight

dresses and go report the hell out of this story," he urged her. "Your crew is here. You need to do this."

"But Superintendent Zimmer—"

"Agrees with me," Dawson said. Before they'd gotten it under control, the fire had nearly consumed them. They were in danger and so was the town. Everyone had to be warned that there was an arsonist on the loose. And not giving him any attention had only made him more dangerous. Maybe if they gave him what he wanted he'd get cocky, slip up and reveal himself.

She released a shaky breath. "Okay, I'll do it."

He picked her up.

"Are you taking me to the firehouse?" she asked.

But he didn't head toward the front door. He headed toward the bathroom. "After you get cleaned up," he said. After he made love to her...

His bathroom was small—barely enough room for two. He held her while he leaned in and turned on the shower. She shrieked when some of the cold spray struck her.

She wriggled and slid down his body. But there was no room for her to back away from him. She was flush against his front—against his straining erection. He pulled off her shirt and shoved down her pants. Then he undressed, too, dropping his soot-saturated clothes atop hers.

She drew in a shaky breath. She skimmed her fingertips across this chest. "The smoke got through your clothes."

He traced a circle across her breast. "Yours, too."

If he hadn't gotten to her when he had...

He shuddered to think what would have happened to her—how tragically he would have lost her. He wrapped his arms around her and pulled her into the shower with him. The warm spray stung his back—while he focused on her front. He soaped up his hands and slid them over her body, washing away the soot. Leaving her golden skin clean and silky again…

She took the soap from him, and he reached for the shampoo, squirting a liberal glob into her hair. As the suds washed out, so did the smoke, streaking over her body to disappear down the drain beneath his feet.

He tensed as her soapy hands ran over his body. She started at his shoulders then skimmed her palms down his arms before coming back for his chest. After soaping up his muscles, she moved her hands lower—across his abs—to his straining erection. She wrapped both hands around him, sliding them up and down.

A groan tore from his throat. She was so damn passionate. So generous. But he wanted to please her, too. So he gritted his teeth and focused on her again. He moved his hands over her breasts. He cupped them in his palms while he teased the nipples with his thumbs.

She moaned and arched into him. So he lifted her high enough that she could slide down onto his erection. He braced his back against the shower and thrust up, filling her.

She pressed her mouth to his shoulder, kissing his skin before nipping gently at it. He didn't know if she was holding in a cry of pleasure or something else—something she wanted to say.

He wanted to say it, too. He wanted to declare his love. But he couldn't give her that burden—he couldn't ask her to stay. No matter what she said Northern Lakes wasn't home.

She bucked, riding him as he thrust. They matched their rhythm as they had so many times before—moving in sync. She came first, though, her orgasm shuddering through her and flowing over him.

And despite her efforts to hold it in, a scream slipped out between her lips. Then he pulled out—just in time. He yelled her name as he came. But he held back the rest. He held in the *I love you.*

Because there was no point in telling her how he felt when they had no future. She had to go back to Chicago. And he had to catch the arsonist.

21

FROM HER APARTMENT, Avery could catch a glimpse of Lake Michigan—if she angled her neck and peered between two other buildings. It wasn't like the view from the deck of her cottage over the lake just feet away.

But the deck was gone. So was the cottage.

So was she.

She'd come back to Chicago. To her job. And to job offers from other markets after the story she'd broken. She'd reported the real cause of the Northern Lakes fire. And for the first time, she'd made herself part of the story. She'd reported how the arsonist had threatened and tried to kill her because he wanted attention. And she'd talked again about the heroism of the Hotshot who hadn't just saved her nephews, but her, as well.

She should have been thrilled with all the opportunities the story had opened for her. She wouldn't have to worry about getting airtime anymore. Her career had never been as promising as it was now.

But she sat alone in her apartment. She didn't feel like celebrating—not when she couldn't be with the people she loved.

She placed a call and held out her cell phone, watching the screen as she waited. Finally a voice emanated from the speaker.

"Hey, Babs," Kim greeted her. "Didn't think you'd have time for us little people anymore."

Her heart ached with missing the little people. And one very big, sexy person.

"Babs?" she asked.

"Everyone in Northern Lakes is comparing you to Barbara Walters," Kim said. "And Oprah."

She laughed as she imagined the old guys down at the coffee shop talking about her.

"It's not just people in Northern Lakes, though," Kim said. "Other networks aired your story, too."

The news was partly why she'd called. Dawson and the Huron Hotshots had been sent out West to battle a never-ending blaze—the one that had already claimed the life of one Hotshot. Arson hadn't started it, Mother Nature had.

"Speaking of news," she said, "have you heard any about the Hotshots?"

"About all of them?" Kim asked. "Or one in particular?"

Avery expelled a ragged sigh. "Okay, I'm worried about Dawson. He never had a break before they sent him out again." He'd never had a chance to recover— or to see her again after that night they'd made love in his shower. Her body ached for his. But her heart ached even more.

"He's tough," Kim assured her. "He'll survive and come back stronger than ever."

She knew Kim was right. Dawson was the strongest man she knew. He would survive. But would she survive missing him?

"I don't know how you do this," Avery said. "With Rick being gone so much…"

"I'm not so pathetic anymore?" Kim asked.

"I never said you were."

"You've thought it," Kim said. "I've seen it on your face."

"Nobody sees anything on my face," Avery said defensively. "I'm a reporter. I never give away my personal feelings."

Kim laughed. "That feature you did on Dawson gave away your feelings. You gave them away even more when you reported how he'd saved you from the arsonist. You love him."

"I…" Couldn't deny it. "I never said you were pathetic. I never thought it, either."

"But you didn't understand how I could be happy marrying young and having a family," Kim said.

"I didn't understand because I never felt what you feel for Rick," Avery said.

"Now you do."

She felt it now. She loved Dawson Hess.

"But how are you happy with Rick?" Avery wondered. "When you're apart so much?" It had only been a week and she couldn't handle it—couldn't focus on her job, on anything but how badly she missed Dawson.

"Missing someone is easier when you know for certain they're coming home," Kim explained. "And when he gets home, we make up for that time apart…"

Avery could sense Kim's sexy smile through the phone. And finally she understood why her sister was so happy. She didn't have Rick all the time, but she had it all with him. The love. The commitment. And the passion.

"What about you?" Kim asked. "When are you coming home?"

She sighed. "I didn't get any job offers in Northern Lakes." Because they didn't even have their own television station. But the ones she'd wanted from New York and LA had come in—along with so many others.

"I didn't say you needed to come home to stay," Kim said. "I know that wouldn't work for you. But you could do what Rick does. He's gone for a week and then comes home for a few days. You don't mind flying. You could work anywhere and still come home to Northern Lakes. To Dawson…"

But did Dawson want her coming home to him? They'd had an incredible week together. But she'd also driven him crazy with her questions, with exposing his life in that special feature. He hated reporters. And while she knew he didn't hate her, she didn't know if he loved her—the way she loved him.

SHE'D GOTTEN HER STORY. It was all she'd wanted. He hadn't heard from her since she'd returned to Chicago. Not a phone call. Or a text or email.

Plenty of other women had contacted him—through the firehouse—since that feature had aired.

They wanted to meet him. Wanted to make him dinner. Take him to bed.

His body ached for release. But there was only one woman he wanted.

Something hard jabbed his leg. He glanced down to see the end of the barbell pushing against it. He was supposed to be spotting Cody. "Need help?" he asked.

Cody easily shoved the barbell up. "Lucky for me I didn't. I'd be choked to death under the bar with you spotting me."

"Sorry," he said. Out West he'd forced himself to focus on the job. But now that they were back in Northern Lakes, he couldn't stop thinking about Avery. She was everywhere—even while she was really hundreds of miles away.

Everyone talked about her, about that amazing Avery Kincaid. If the arsonist had intended to get attention from her broadcast, he had to be disappointed. She was the one who'd gotten all the attention. Well, not all the attention.

He had all those offers from random women. Even a few men...

So why had nothing happened since Avery left? Was she the arsonist's total focus now—as she was Dawson's? The whole time they'd been out West they'd been worrying, but Northern Lakes was safe. Was Avery?

"You're pathetic," Cody said with a snort of disgust.

Dawson had just bench-pressed more than the younger guy had. "What the hell are you talking about?"

Cody shook his head. "Can't believe you and Wyatt—falling like schmucks for these hot chicks."

He wanted to deny it, wanted to claim he hadn't fallen. But he would never lie to one of the crew. He might keep something from them. But he wouldn't lie.

"I'm sick of you moping around here," Cody said.

"We only just got back to Northern Lakes," Dawson reminded him.

"You shouldn't be here," Braden chimed in.

Dawson hadn't even been aware that their boss had joined them in the workout room.

Zimmer continued, "You shouldn't be in Northern Lakes right now."

Dawson had been so worried about Avery that he'd been oblivious to what was going on in his own life. Had something changed? The tension in his body spread to his head, making it pound.

Was Zimmer kicking him off the team?

"I thought you didn't have a problem with my working with Wyatt," he said. Even after Avery's special report, they'd worked together the same as they always had.

"I don't," Zimmer said. "I have a problem with one of my guys being so upset."

"We're all upset," Dawson said. "We want the arsonist caught."

"You're not upset over the arsonist," Zimmer said.

"Yes—"

"You're upset over the hot reporter," Cody said.

He just shrugged. "Maybe that's why the arsonist hasn't hit anything in Northern Lakes again. Because she's gone."

"So you think it's good she's gone?"

He shook his head. "I think the arsonist could have followed her back to Chicago."

"Then what the hell are you doing here?" Zimmer asked.

He tensed. It was true. If Avery was in danger, he needed to be with her—needed to protect her. "I need some time off," he said. "I need to go to Chicago."

Cody laughed. "It's about damn time."

"Why are you going?" Zimmer asked.

"I just told you, she could be in danger—"

"Or not," Zimmer said. "She's not the only one who hasn't been in town."

Cody sucked in a breath as realization dawned. "We haven't been."

"None of the fires have happened while we've been gone," Braden pointed out.

"Son of a bitch," Dawson cursed. It had felt personal to him; he just hadn't realized how personal. "We're the ones he's after." Sure, he'd gone after Avery, too, but

that had probably been because Dawson had been seeing her—getting her attention.

Zimmer nodded.

The other two men looked tense. Dawson was relieved.
Maybe Avery *was* safe.

"Are you still going?" Cody asked.

"To Chicago?" If she wasn't in danger, he had no excuse to go. Except the most important one of all—he
loved her. "Hell, yes."

"Be careful," Zimmer warned as he started out the
door. "Watch your back."

The arsonist hadn't tried anything with them individu-
ally. He set the fires to take on the entire crew. The only
individual he'd targeted was Avery.

Was that because of Dawson, though?

The arsonist had been watching her, so he'd known
how often Dawson had gone to see her—how he felt
about her. Had being with Avery put her in danger?

Then maybe he shouldn't go see her...

He was still debating as he drove back to his cabin.
He didn't want to put her in danger. But he wanted to see
her. He needed to see her. To be with her...

And if the arsonist was fixated on all the Hotshots, he
would stay here—where the majority of them were. He
wouldn't follow Dawson to Chicago.

Was she still there? Her special reports had to have
received the attention of the networks. She could move
to New York. Or LA. It had only been a week, but maybe
she already had.

Before he booked his flight, he would check with her
sister. Kim would know where she was.

He pulled the truck up next to his cabin and killed the
engine. Then he jumped out and slammed the driver's

door. The sound echoed around the woods—what was left of the woods after that damn fire.

He was lucky the arsonist hadn't hit his side of the forest. Just Cody's.

Maybe he'd offer to let Cody stay at his place until he got back. He crossed the short front porch and reached for the door. But he didn't have to push it open; it already stood open.

Since their return to Northern Lakes the day before, he'd been back to the cabin. Surely he hadn't been so distracted he'd left the door open. Or unlocked.

He glanced around again, but only his truck sat in the driveway. There were no other vehicles. If someone had broken in, they'd come on foot.

Why would someone do that?

Because they didn't want anyone seeing their vehicle and maybe getting the license plate number?

He pushed the door open a little farther. The door creaked, but another creak inside echoed it. And he saw a shadow falling across the floor.

Someone had broken into his place. And he could think of only one reason why. The arsonist intended to burn down Dawson's place now.

22

AVERY SHIVERED WITH FEAR. While she still considered Northern Lakes home, it didn't feel the way it had before. It wasn't the safe and happy place it had once been to her.

It was the place the arsonist had nearly killed her—not once but twice. The first time he'd only been trying to scare her enough to tell his story. The second time he'd been so angry he'd wanted her dead. And he would have killed her if it wasn't for Dawson.

She heard a creak, but before she could turn around strong arms grabbed her, holding her tight. She screamed. Then she recognized the arms, the musky scent.

"Dawson."

Instead of loosening, his grasp on her tightened and he murmured, "I can't believe it's you."

She struggled slightly, just enough that she could turn around in his arms. "I wanted to surprise you," she said.

He expelled a shaky breath. "You surprised me, all right. There's no other car around and you left the door open."

"I had Kim drop me off so I could surprise you." A pang of regret struck her. "I'm sorry. I should have known better. I should have known you might not be happy to see me." After all, he had never really forgiven her for the report she'd done on him.

He touched her face, his fingers skimming along her jaw and then over her lips. "Shh…" he said. "I'm very happy it's you."

"Oh." Her breath escaped in a gasp. "You thought it was the arsonist waiting in here. I'm sorry—"

His fingers brushed over her lips again, stilling them. "I forgive you," he said.

And hope swelled in her heart. She didn't think he was talking about surprising him as she just had. "You do?"

He nodded.

"But I didn't think you could," she said. "You were so mad at me."

"I got over being mad at you a long time ago," he said.

Had he gotten over her, too? Or had he never really been into her? Not like she was into him. Having Kim drop her off had been a horrible idea. Not only had she alarmed him, but she'd also trapped herself. If he rejected the declaration of love she intended to make, she couldn't escape with a quick exit. She would have to suffer through her humiliation while he drove her home. If he would drive her home…

"I'm sorry," she said again. "I shouldn't have ignored your wishes."

"No, you shouldn't have," he agreed.

He didn't exactly sound as if he'd forgiven her.

"I can't take that back," she said. The report had taken on a life of its own now. "But I can respect your wishes from now on."

She stared up at him. She'd missed him so much. All she wanted was to throw her arms around his neck and pull his head down for a kiss. But if she kissed him, they would make love. And they wouldn't talk.

While she had never had much success in getting Dawson to talk before, she had to now. She had to learn how he felt. So she asked, "What do you wish for?"

And she held her breath while she waited for his answer.

DAWSON WISHED FOR many things. He wished they knew who the arsonist was. He wished that she and everyone in Northern Lakes would be safe. But more than that he wished she loved him.

Answering questions was never easy for him, though. Especially when he didn't know why she was asking them. "What is this?" he asked. "A follow-up interview?"

"A follow-up?" she repeated. "You would've had to grant me an interview in the first place. But you didn't."

"It didn't stop you."

Hurt and regret flashed in her turquoise eyes. She really did feel bad about having run the story. So she wasn't interviewing him again.

"I'm sorry," he said now. "I'm really not angry about that anymore."

"You're bitter instead," she said, and there was a hopelessness in her voice he'd never heard before.

She was always so determined, so optimistic.

"And you'll never trust me," she continued. "I shouldn't have come here. This was a mistake." She moved as if to tug free of his loose embrace, her hands braced against his chest. But he tightened his arms around her; he wasn't going to let her go.

"I'm the one making the mistake," he said. He was screwing up his chance with her. But first he had to know if he had a chance. "I haven't heard from you in more than a week—"

"I didn't hear from you either," she interrupted.

He smiled at her defensiveness. "I've been a little busy fighting fires out West."

"I know…"

He asked the question that had been bothering him. "Why haven't you been covering those stories?"

She shrugged. "A certain Hotshot pointed out to me how reporters just tend to get in the way and make a firefighter's job more dangerous."

"True," he agreed. "You make my job more dangerous even when you're not there."

The hurt was in her eyes again. "How?"

"Because you distract me," he said. "You're all I've thought about…"

"You can't afford to be distracted," she said. Alarm and concern replaced the hurt. "Not with how dangerous your job is."

"I know." He'd done his job, but he hadn't been as focused as he usually was. Because of her…

"What are you going to do about it?" she asked.

"Zimmer gave me a few days off to get my head together." Actually to get together with her.

"How were you planning to do that?"

"By going to Chicago and seeing you," he said.

Her beautiful eyes brightened with hope, and she smiled. "You were coming to see me?"

"Just stopped back here to pack," he said.

She moved her hands over his chest. "You wouldn't have needed any clothes."

"I thought about that." He slid his hands down her back to her hips and pulled her a little closer. His body ached for hers, his erection throbbing behind his fly. "But if I hadn't stopped back here, I would have missed you."

She laughed. "Like star-crossed lovers…" Then the brightness in her eyes dimmed. "Maybe we are star-crossed. How can we make this work? We're both so busy."

"We are both busy people," he agreed. "But every chance we get we'll be together. Every break I'll come to you—wherever you are."

"You don't want me to move back to Northern Lakes?"

"And do what?" he asked with a derisive snort. "Report on the local bake sales? No. I want you to be you— the hotshot reporter I fell in love with."

She gasped, and her eyes widened with shock. And hope. And something else… Something he hoped he wasn't just imagining. Her voice quavering slightly, she asked, "You love me?"

"With all my heart," he said. "And because of that, I will never stand in the way of your career. I'll support you."

"You gave me the greatest story of my career," she said.

"The arsonist?"

She tensed, as if just the mention of him scared her.

"Don't worry," he assured her. "We think it may be our team he has the problem with. Not you."

"That doesn't make me feel any better."

"We'll catch him," he promised. "We'll stop him."

"I believe you."

"I'm glad you did the story," he said. "I'm glad you informed the public about him. But I'm happiest about what it's done for your career."

"I have job offers from all over," she said.

"For more investigative reporting?"

"Some," she said.

But she didn't sound as excited about that as he'd thought she would be.

"One network wants me to do more special reports,"

she said, with more enthusiasm. "Like what I did about you. It's out of New York City."

"I like New York."

"You do?" she asked.

"It's a nice change of pace from here."

"From snail to breakneck?"

He laughed. "It'll be a good balance."

Her breath shuddered out in a sigh of relief. "I'll have more free time," she said. "With doing the special reports, I'll be able to come home often. I'm having the cottage rebuilt, too—making it a year-round home."

He smiled. She had already decided how to make a relationship between them work. "And I'll be with you every chance I get."

She smiled, too.

"I'm glad something good came of all the destruction the arsonist has caused," he said.

"Him—the fire—that wasn't the greatest story of my career," she said.

"What was?" he asked.

"You," she said. "You're a hero. My hero."

He had never wanted to be anyone's hero. He'd only wanted to do his job. Until now. Until Avery. He wanted to be her hero. He wanted to be her everything.

"I love you," she said.

He released a ragged sigh of relief.

"How could you not know?" she asked. "Kim and Fiona said I gave away my feelings in the report about you."

"You loved me then?"

She nodded. "Before I even met you, I loved you for saving my nephews. Then when I met you, I couldn't help falling even more in love with you."

"I tried to fight my feelings," he admitted.

She slapped his chest lightly.

"But you're persistent, Ms. Kincaid," he said. "I didn't have a chance."

But they did. Their love was so strong that their relationship could survive anything: an arsonist, busy careers, separations…

And every time they reunited, the attraction would be as hot as the first time they'd met. He reached for the buttons on her blouse as she tugged up his shirt. In seconds nothing separated them—they were skin to skin. Heart to heart…

* * * * *

Hotshot Cody Mallehan doesn't get attached to any place or anyone. But beautiful Serena Beaumont might just tempt him to stay in Northern Lakes— and in her bed—forever…

Look for HOT SEDUCTION (September 2016), the next installment in Lisa Childs's HOTSHOT HEROES miniseries.

COMING NEXT MONTH FROM

HARLEQUIN *Blaze*

Available April 19, 2016

#891 DARING HER SEAL
Uniformly Hot!
by Anne Marsh
DEA agent Ashley Dixon and Navy SEAL Levi Brandon are
shocked to discover their faux wedding from their last mission
was legitimate. They don't even like each other! Which doesn't
mean they aren't hot for each other...

#892 COME CLOSER, COWBOY
Made in Montana
by Debbi Rawlins
Hollywood transplant Mallory Brandt is opening a new bar in
Blackfoot Falls. She needs a fresh start, but sexy stuntman
Gunner Ellison is determined to remind her of the past...one
amazing night in particular.

#893 BIG SKY SEDUCTION
by Daire St. Denis
When uptight Gloria Hurst sleeps with laid-back cowboy
Dillon Cross, she does what any control freak would do—pretend
it never happened. But a moment of weakness is quickly turning
into something that could last a lifetime!

#894 THE FLYBOY'S TEMPTATION
by Kimberly Van Meter
Former Air Force pilot J.T. Carmichael knew Dr. Hope Larsen's
request to fly into the Mexican jungle came with a mess of
complications. But when they're stranded, the heat between
them becomes too hard to resist...

"Can you be married without having sex?"

Levi Brandon's SEAL team leader, Gray Jackson, slapped him on the back, harder than was strictly necessary. "Last time I checked, you weren't married, planning on getting married or even dating the same woman for consecutive nights. The better question is... can you go without having sex?"

He'd tried dating when he was younger. Hell. The word *younger* made him feel like Methuselah, but the feeling wasn't inaccurate. Courtesy of Uncle Sam, he'd seen plenty and done more. The civilian women he'd dated once upon a time didn't understand what his job entailed.

He certainly had no plans for celibacy. On the other hand, fate had just slapped him with the moral equivalent of a chastity belt. Levi pulled the marriage certificate out of a pocket of his flight suit and waved it at his team.

Sam unfolded the paper, read it over and whistled. "You're married?"

"Not on purpose," Levi admitted with a scowl.

HBEXP0416

Mason held out a hand for the certificate. "When did this happen?"

"I'm blaming you." Mason was a big bear of a SEAL, a damned good sniper and the second member of their unit to find *true love* when they'd been undercover on Fantasy Island three months ago. "Your girl asked Ashley and me to be the stand-in bride and groom for a beach ceremony. She didn't tell us we were getting married for real."

Mason grinned. "Heads up. Every photo shoot with that woman is an adventure."

"Yeah," he grumbled, "but can you really imagine me married? To *Ashley*?"

Ashley Dixon had been a DEA tagalong on their past two missions. As far as he could tell, she disliked everything about him—she'd been happy to detail her opinions loudly and at length. Naturally he'd given her plenty of shit while they'd been in their field together, and she'd *really* hated him calling her Mrs. Brandon after they'd played bride and groom for Mason's girl.

After they'd parted ways on Fantasy Island, he hadn't thought of her once. Okay. He'd thought of her once. Maybe twice. She was gorgeous, they had a little history together and he wasn't dead yet, although he was fairly certain he *would* be if he pursued her. But how the hell had he ended up married to her?

Don't miss DARING HER SEAL
by New York Times *bestselling author Anne Marsh,*
available May 2016 wherever
Harlequin® Blaze® books and ebooks are sold.

www.Harlequin.com